Blood of the Innocent

by

Cheryel Hutton

The Lobster Cove Series

Blood of the Innocent

Cover Art by *Debbie Taylor*

The Wild Rose Press, Inc.
PO Box 708
Adams Basin, NY 14410-0708
Visit us at www.thewildrosepress.com

Publishing History
First Black Rose Edition, 2015
Print ISBN 978-1-5092-0408-3
Digital ISBN 978-1-5092-0409-0

The Lobster Cove Series
Published in the United States of America

"I'm sorry. I was coming out here to ask what you take in your coffee."

"I prefer black." He couldn't resist reaching out to touch the silky blonde hair that flowed down her back all the way to her perfectly shaped ass. He could get lost just looking at her. What would it be like to hold her close, to kiss her until she melted in his arms? To touch her, taste her, feel her beneath him?

She shot to her feet and backed away from him. "What are you thinking?"

He shrugged. "I'm thinking about the beautiful woman beside me."

Her hand was trembling as she put it over her heart. "But I'm vampire and you're—"

"A man." He rose to his feet and went to her. Her gorgeous sea green eyes widened, but she stood waiting for him.

He slid one hand under her hair, the other around her waist, then nudged her toward him. Sure she'd resist, he was shocked when she leaned against him.

His lips touched her warm, firm, perfect mouth, and he heard himself groan. Then her arms wrapped around his neck, and a soft sigh shot heat straight to his loins.

She leaned into him, and her soft curves fit against him in all the right places. His body hardened, while his thinking processes blurred. He had to have this woman; he had to be inside her. He needed her as much as he needed his next breath.

All at once an image of Justin lying cold and dead on the rocky shoreline rushed into his mind. He shoved Veronica away.

Praise for Cheryel Hutton

"All in all, *KEEPERS OF LEGEND* was a fun little story with a deeper message. Cheryel Hutton has a nice writing style, and I hope to read a longer story by her."

~Ricki, Bitten by Books (3 Stars)

~*~

"As I finished reading *KEEPERS OF LEGEND* I had one wish; I would have loved the story to go on longer. There was huge potential for the story to continue with its tale of dragons and love. This is not to say *KEEPERS OF LEGEND* wasn't a finished tale. It most definitely was, but I was left with a yearning for more of the tale of Simon and his human friends."

~Orchid, Long and Short Reviews (4.5 Books)

~*~

"This is the second book in a series. I didn't realize this was the case when I requested it, but I had no problem at all getting caught up on the most important details of previous events within a chapter or two. It can definitely be read as a standalone work, and that made me happy. *SECRETS OF UGLY CREEK* is a good choice for anyone who likes science fiction whose setting is completely humdrum and ordinary."

~Astilbe, Long and Short Reviews (3 Stars)

Dedication

To my wonderful daughters, Amanda and Carrie
(in alphabetical order).
Thank you, both of you, for being so supportive.
Love you two!

Chapter 1

The sweet, tangy smell of blood filled the night air, and Veronica took a moment to enjoy the scent before she shoved the feeling into the recesses of her mind. It wouldn't do for the humans to see hunger in her face.

As soon as she was sure she was in control, she turned from where she'd pulled her Lexus behind a marked police car. A breeze off Frenchman Bay brushed over her and she heard the soft roar of waves battering the rocky shore. Just above the rocks, where there was still soil and foliage, an artificially lighted spot churned with uniformed police.

As she'd expected, one of the Bar Harbor police officers stepped toward her. "Sorry, you can't go any farther."

"I'm expected," she told him, holding out her credentials. "I'm a consultant for the FBI."

The officer, who wasn't much taller than she was, glanced at the badge, then back at her face. "We don't get a lot of murders here, but we can handle them when we do."

She didn't blame him for being hesitant. "I'm not an agent. Like I said, I'm here as a consultant."

"Like I said, nobody told me."

She was just about to *convince* the officer, when a familiar woman approached them. Veronica let out a relieved sigh. "Hello, Pat."

The tall, warm-skinned human wore a long, yellow dress draped gracefully over one shoulder, a pair of beat-up sneakers, and purple latex gloves. Even in eveningwear, there was no missing the authority emanating from the formidable Pat Hutchins. "Let her through, dumbass." Pat glared at the officer.

Pat led Veronica through a line of tall pines, down a steep stone wall, and onto a rocky shore. The ubiquitous Maine fog thickened with every passing moment, reflecting back the harsh lights used to pierce the darkness. Veronica had no problem moving over the jutting and slick rocks. While trying to look like she couldn't see her way any better than anyone else, she kept an eye out for any difficulties her human friend had. The Maine-born coroner was used to the terrain, and the fog, so Veronica's vigilance was unneeded. "So you were at a formal event when they called you?"

"I actually dared go to the opera with a couple of friends. You think I'd know better."

"Sorry, Pat. You deserved the night off."

She sighed. "Isn't that the truth."

About two-thirds of the way to the lapping waves, the body of a human male sprawled over the rocks. One arm lay across the man's chest, the other to the side, as if he was reaching for help while he died.

The body, she'd guess the age to be early thirties, was the source of the blood smell. His throat had been sliced open, resulting in splatter over his face, body, the rocks around him, and presumably his attacker.

Still, even though the gory substance covered the man's neck, chest, and rocks around him, she was sure it wasn't the huge amount that would be lost in seconds when both carotid arteries were severed. He'd have lost much more.

"He appears to have only been dead a couple of hours," Pat said.

Veronica nodded at the verification of what she already knew, what she'd been fearful of since Pat had texted her. The man was the victim of one of her kind. As if to confirm the facts, a slight movement of air filled her nose with the fading scent of one of her own. "Damn."

"I was correct in my assessment?"

Veronica nodded. "Thanks for calling me."

"Are you kidding, I need your help on this."

"You know I'll do all I can." She looked into her friend's concerned eyes. She couldn't blame Pat. She was worried herself.

"I want to see him!"

Veronica looked toward the shout to see a man pull away from the uniformed officers and stumble toward them. As he moved through the gray wall of fog, he looked so much like the dead man, it almost seemed as if the body had come to life. Same dark hair, long legs, broad shoulders. Pat stepped toward the man. "Sir, you need—"

He sidestepped the medical examiner's reach, falling to one knee as he did. It only took him a heartbeat to get back to his feet and continue his stumbling trek across the rocky shore toward Veronica. She could have stopped him, but that would provoke questions she couldn't answer. Besides, she understood his need to see and understand. Holding him back would just cause him more pain.

The man got a good look at the body and jerked to a stop. "Justin. *No!*" the horror-filled words were nothing compared to the anguish on his face.

He lunged toward the body, and this time she did stop him. "I can't let you contaminate the scene," she told him.

"That's my brother!"

"I'm so sorry." Pat said, as she came up beside him and put a hand on his shoulder.

He closed his eyes, and leaned over to put his hands on his thighs, like a runner with a cramp. Veronica thought he might collapse, but he got hold of himself and straightened his back. "What happened?"

"That's what we're trying to find out," Pat told him.

The man groaned. "He can't be dead. He can't."

"I'm so sorry," Pat said again. "Now please go and let us do our job."

His head and shoulders dropped as if deflated. A uniformed cop took the man's arm and escorted him back past the line of pine trees.

"Poor guy," Pat said. "Losing his brother like that. Apparently his twin brother too."

"Looks that way," Veronica agreed, before they both turned back to their work.

Sitting on her heels beside the body, she swiped the all but invisible second, smaller cut just below the almost ear-to-ear slash across the victim's throat. She inserted the swab into a sterile vial, sealed and labeled it, then took another sample from the other side of the longer gash, put the second swab in another vial, and labeled that one too.

"I can get you an uncontaminated sample of the victim's blood."

Veronica smiled at the woman. "Thank you. That

would be very helpful."

"Sure. If you need anything else, just let me know."

Samples taken, pictures shot, notes written, Veronica stood. "I'll get out of your way. Good luck with your investigation."

"Keep me in the loop."

"Will do." Her stomach twisted with the obligation to lie, to hold information back from a person she liked and admired—and who needed every shred of data she could get to solve a murder. Not that the police had any hope of catching the killer. The perpetrator of this crime wasn't human.

Veronica smiled at her friend, then turned and headed deftly across the rocks toward her car. As she climbed the steep slope toward the line of pines at the top, a crime scene van pulled in. Several evidence specialists gathered equipment in anticipation of working the area. She sighed, hopeful they would find something useful, though she knew they wouldn't.

A contingent of uniformed police officers and a couple of detectives in plain clothes stood restlessly at the place where the rocks became a steep incline down to the beach. "We don't need Feds sticking their noses in our local business," one of the officers said. The guy who'd stopped her earlier stood nearby glaring.

Veronica included both men in her gaze. "I'm only a consultant. You have nothing to worry about."

"Consultant on what?"

"I'm a biochemist working on variations in blood. I look for unusual characteristics as a way of identifying suspects." The memorized spiel was just close enough to the truth to be believable. She hoped.

The closer officer rubbed his chin. "Sounds experimental."

"It is, right now. In a few years it'll probably be standard procedure." If the higher-ups on both sides of the human-vampire line took politics out of the equation and thought about the bigger picture.

"You go right ahead and play with your test tubes. Just stay the hell out of our way. Understand?"

"Perfectly." She gave him a sarcastic smile, and he narrowed his eyes.

Either feeling he'd made his point, or that she was hopeless, he turned and headed toward the body. Veronica ignored the other cops and walked away as fast as she could without drawing attention to herself. Every passing moment brought sunrise closer, and she needed to get home before she got into real trouble.

The sound of footsteps behind her sent twinges of irritation up her spine. All she wanted to do was go home, where she was safe from the sun, and relax. Maybe if she ignored whoever was behind her he'd go away.

"So you work for the FBI?"

It was the victim's brother. Damn, she couldn't just tell the man to get lost. He was in a lot of emotional pain—she could feel it washing over her like a wave of icy water. She looked at him. "Only as a consultant."

"Why does the FBI need a consultant on my brother's murder?"

"It's not this case in particular."

"Then why aren't the police accustomed to you being around."

She should have realized this would be difficult. A glance at the sky told her she treaded dangerous waters.

Why was it she had thought it was a good idea to move to the place that received the first taste of sunrise every morning? "I don't have time to explain right now. Why don't you check with the coroner later?"

"And let you vanish into the Federal ether?

"I live in Lobster Cove. I'll be around." She got into her car, only to find a male hand holding the top of the door. Not that she couldn't close it anyway, but that would cause problems she didn't have time to deal with. Reaching into her purse, she pulled out a small notebook and scribbled down her cell number. She shoved the small sheet of paper at the man. "Now let me go, I'm late for an appointment."

He took the paper and stepped back. She hadn't turned her car around before her phone rang. "Teal."

"Just wanted to make sure you gave me your real number."

She glared in her rearview as she clicked off her cell. This dude would be a thorn in her side if she wasn't careful. That didn't matter right now, though. All that mattered was getting home before the sun became dangerous.

By the time she'd parked her car and raced up the walkway toward the sunny yellow, renovated Georgian style house, her face and hands tingled. She flung open the front door, rushed inside, and ran for the staircase.

Careful to avoid any sun's rays that peeked through the big first floor window and onto the steps, she tore into her apartment and shut the solid wooden door behind her. With a sigh of relief, she went to the specially coated window in her living room. From the safety of her own space, she stood at the little round table in front of the window and watched the sun rise over the horizon. The tops of her hands and her face stung. She looked down at the reddened areas on her hands, and thought about how just a few more minutes would have meant severe damage, and the need for medical care. A few more after that, and the burns would be life-threatening. The consequences of sunlight for a vampire.

Her thoughts turned to the dead man on the Bar Harbor shore, and his distraught brother. He thought he could get answers from her, but her role in the death was almost finished. Once she ran the samples and turned the results over to the Guardians, she'd probably never know anything more.

Not knowing had never bothered her before, but today she found herself wondering about the events that had led up to the human's demise. What was the name his brother had used? Justin, that was it. Similar to justice. Would Justin get justice? Would his brother ever know if he did?

As she turned toward a long, hot soak in the tub, another question tugged at her. What would Justin's brother think if he knew his twin had been killed by a being whose kind had spawned legends? And that the woman he looked to for answers was one of them. Creatures dependent on human blood for survival. Feared and hated through history. Hunter and hunted.

Vampire.

Chapter 2

Joe Sullivan's hand shook as he inserted the key and twisted the knob, but when he tried to open the door it wouldn't budge. For a moment he had a powerful urge to kick the damn thing in.

When he managed to get hold of himself, he twisted the key in the opposite direction. The knob turned. Maybe he'd been wrong about the direction, but he'd heard the lock click. The truth smacked him hard. The door had been unlocked. Dreading what he'd find, he pushed the door open.

From where he stood, he could see his brother's apartment was a wreck. Books, papers, photos, even couch cushions, covered the floor. Through the open door into the bedroom, he could see clothing hanging from open drawers, and the bare mattress where it stood propped against the wall.

Joe closed his eyes for a moment in an effort to contain the anger roaring inside him. The knowledge that Justin would never walk in the door again was bad enough, but the idea of strangers digging through his brother's things flared a need to beat the shit out of somebody. Anybody.

He had only been to this apartment twice, once to help Justin move in, and then again almost a year ago. Maine and Tennessee were over a thousand miles from each other, which made it harder to fit visits into their busy schedules.

Busy schedules! Damn it to hell. If he'd only looked beyond how busy he was and made an effort, maybe his brother wouldn't be lying bloody and cold on a beach far away from home.

The image that flashed in his head brought bile into his throat. He rushed into the bathroom, dropped to his knees, and waited for his body to stop convulsing. There really wasn't anything to throw up. He hadn't eaten since, how long was it? Twenty-four hours, maybe? After Justin had called, all he could think of was to get to his brother as fast as he could. Just not fast enough.

Finally he was able to stand and flush the toilet. He had to remove the scattered contents of the medicine cabinet from the sink before he could wash out his mouth and splash water on his face. Before he was finished, sobs wracked him.

A few long minutes later, he managed to clean himself up and stumbled into his brother's kitchen. Like the rest of the place, this room was trashed. Food, dishes, pots, everything was strewn over the counters, stove, and sink. The fridge was open, leaving food to rot and milk to sour. Justin would be livid if he saw this.

Joe slammed the fridge door closed, rattling the cabinets. This wasn't possible. No way could his brilliant, dynamic, incredible twin be gone. It couldn't be.

He located the coffeemaker, only to find it hadn't been cleaned since the last time it was used. That told him a lot. Justin was a clean freak, so he had to have left in a major hurry.

Taking a deep breath, Joe calmed himself enough to dump out the grounds and clean the machine. Once the coffee was done and he located a mug, he took the drink into the living room and stood by the window.

Who the hell would want to hurt a man as caring and even-tempered as his brother? Had Justin somehow gotten himself mixed up in something bad enough to put his life at risk? It seemed impossible, but his twin had been worried when he called, and something had happened that resulted in his brother's death. Joe's heart twisted. How could he deal with the loss of the person who was more than a brother? They were more like two parts of a whole.

He thought back to their weekly conversations. For almost a month, his brother had sounded strange, worried. Joe had questioned him about specifics, but Justin would only tell him that he was on the trail of a big story and didn't want to talk about it yet. Joe hadn't been concerned. His journalist brother didn't discuss anything until he was good and ready.

When he'd called to say he was in trouble, that he'd happened on a conspiracy, it had shaken Joe. Whatever Justin had discovered, it had to be serious for him to admit concern.

He'd spoken of some sort of creature that looked human but wasn't. It was impossible to believe something so unrealistic could exist, but Justin had insisted they did. He'd also insisted some of the creatures were good, honest, caring folks; and something in his brother's voice had Joe suspecting he'd gotten close to one of them.

Justin said the whatevers had enormous psychic abilities and that most couldn't be trusted. He'd been rushed, saying he had to go somewhere, that a source had something important to tell him. Before he hung up, though, he'd said the humans involved were more dangerous than the non-humans. He wasn't sure who to trust, he'd said, except someone he called "C". He said he'd call Joe when he got home. "Don't bother," Joe had told him, I'm coming to you.

He hadn't believed that these wannabe humans existed, but he knew if his brother was worried, he had a reason. Joe had grabbed the next flight from Tennessee to Maine, only to find he was much too late. His brother was gone.

Joe groaned and rubbed his forehead. The whole thing was crazy, totally bat-shit insane. Then again, Justin was lying dead on a rocky shoreline more than a thousand miles from home. Nothing could be crazier than that.

Was this conspiracy, this whatever-it-was involving "creatures," was that what got his brother killed? Did one of the conspiracy nuts decide he knew too much? Was it possible there was something to this non-human thing?

His head buzzing with unanswered questions, he swallowed the rest of the coffee and sat the cup on a small table near the window. He needed answers, so he went into his brother's bedroom to begin checking hiding places only a twin would be able to find.

****

The next night at the lab was long and hard. Veronica decided walking home would be a good idea, and the exercise and fresh air did help her clear her mind. As she neared her apartment, she looked forward to a quiet day at home.

Foliage blocked the view from the front of her two-story apartment building, but the sense of another of her kind was strong. It wasn't long before it became obvious who was waiting for her. Unfortunately, the sense went both ways, making it impossible to escape what she knew was coming. The day was not going the way she'd planned.

"Hello, Mom."

Emelda Teal gave Veronica a put-upon look. "I've been waiting for two hours. It's almost dawn, for God's sake! I could have been seriously burned waiting for you. You'd think, since you work for other vampires, they would realize you have to be home by sunrise."

Veronica pulled out her keys to open the main door into the building. "I had a sample to finish. there was enough time to get home before daylight."

Her mother didn't even slow down. "This place is nuts! First town in the United States to get sunrise. What kind of a place is that for vampires?"

Veronica's jaw clenched. This conversation might just be her one proverbial straw too many, and it was all she could do to hang on to her self-control. "You didn't have to move here, Mom."

"I wouldn't be much of a mother if I let both my daughters seek their fortunes in this infernal place and not be close by in case either of you need anything."

"Charlene didn't have to come here either." She regretted saying the words as soon as they came out of her mouth, and tried to cover by opening the front door and heading up the stairs toward her apartment.

"Why did you pick an apartment with all these stairs? Climbing is hard on a woman my age. Although, this is probably why you have such a great figure.

Charlene could do with some stair climbing."

Veronica opened the door and ushered her mother into her sanctuary. "I chose this place because I fell in love with it. The owners managed to upgrade to modern conveniences without losing the charm of the building."

"Why you aren't happy your sister and I moved here is beyond me. I'd think you'd be thrilled to have family nearby. And you know your sister and I believed that if opportunities existed for you here, The same should be true for Charlene. So far that hasn't held true, unfortunately."

Veronica opened her mouth to remind her mother that she'd come for a specific job, not because Maine or Lobster Cove had more opportunities, and Charlene had come for her own reasons. She let it go though, it was a lost cause and she knew it. "Have a seat, Mom. Would you like some tea?"

A knock interrupted her attempt at being cordial. As she turned to answer the door, her mother perked up with obvious curiosity. Veronica smiled when she opened the door. "Hi, Tim, come in and join us." She put a bit of emphasis on the last word.

His eyes widened and he straightened his spine and raised his chin before he stepped into the apartment.

"Mom, this is my friend Tim Hunnicutt from across the hall."

"Pleased to meet you, Mrs. Teal." He took one of the woman's hands and touched his lips to it.

Emelda smiled. "How nice! I thought all the real gentlemen had disappeared."

Tim smiled. "There are a few of us left who subscribe to the more gentle ways." His deep voice exuded a sensuality that could send tingles down a woman's body. Veronica bit back a grin.

Her mother laughed, actually laughed, with a human no less! Veronica's vision blurred and she was bit lightheaded, as if she might be going into shock or something.

"What is it you do for a living, Tim?" Emelda asked.

"I'm a lawyer."

"Really? How interesting."

"Oh, it is very interesting. I work with a nice group of lawyers down in Bar Harbor."

"Your friend is a real gem," Emelda said.

"He's something else, for sure." She tossed a glance at Tim, who only smiled innocently.

"Well," Emelda stood. "I should be going."

Veronica's breath caught, and she moved toward the couch. "Mom, you're welcome to stay here." She met the other woman's gaze and sent a mental message. *The sun's up. What are you thinking?*

I have a hat, gloves, and a wrap, her mother silently replied, then said, "Fernando is picking me up in the limo. I'll be fine."

Veronica knew she had a holy-crap expression on her face, but she decided her mom could think what she wanted as she walked Emelda to the door. Limo? Fernando, the little human with the weak chin?

"No need to walk me out, dear." Emelda took a raincoat, hat, and umbrella from a bag she'd left by Veronica's door. "I'll be fine."

"Be careful, Mom."

Emelda leaned in close. "Too bad he's human."

Veronica nodded, then leaned her head against the closed door. Guess she'd have been fine even if she'd been in the sun for a while after all.

"Your mother's quite a character." The pitch of Tim's voice had risen a good octave.

Veronica turned; smiling at the man now sprawled on her couch. "That she is."

"You haven't told your mother about your best girl friend?" Tim's voice raised another half-octave and his manner had reverted to the outrageously gay one she was used to seeing from her friend.

"I think she wanted to fix me up with you," she said, as she headed toward the kitchen.

"Oh honey, I love you, but you're really not my type."

"Ha-ha." She came back into the room with two bottles of water and handed one to Tim. "You aren't my type either."

"And what type would that be?" The top of the bottle only partly hid his teasing smile.

"B positive," she said, and they both laughed.

"You are positively nuts."

"Thank you."

"So your mom has a boyfriend?"

"Fernando is human."

"God forbid."

Veronica laughed. "Honestly, I don't know what he is to her. I do know he does pretty much what she wants him to do." She shrugged. "She's probably paying him an unholy amount of money to be her...whatever he is

Tim leaned his head to one side. "Or maybe she's into kink and he's her slave."

Her heart went into overdrive and she couldn't catch her breath. Everything seemed to go out of focus, and it took a couple of minutes to get her equilibrium back. "Impossible."

He patted her hand. "Good grief, Veronica. Your mother is a consenting adult. You said yourself that since the divorce she's been acting strange."

"If she's doing kinky stuff with that odd little human, I don't want to know about it."

"Fair enough." He took a strand of her long hair in his hand. "Are you sure you won't let me give you a makeover." He waved a hand up and down her. "I could do wonders with your wardrobe and makeup."

She put a hand on Tim's arm. "I'm not a girly-girl. I don't care much about clothes and makeup."

Hand on chest, he looked at her with sadness in his expression. "Such a waste of perfect features, gorgeous hair, and a wonderful figure. You slay me, darling."

"Funny, Tim. Buffy I'm not."

"That's for sure." He stood. "I gotta go. I have a rehearsal this afternoon."

"Are you still working on that Aretha Franklin song? I thought you had that one down."

His smug expression made her wonder what he was up to. "No, I have a new number I'm working on."

"I can't wait to hear it."

"Soon. I promise."

She walked him to her door. "Break a leg."

"I'll give it my best try." He kissed her cheek and headed across the hall.

Veronica went back into her apartment and headed toward a long, warm, much needed, relaxing bath.

****

Making the call home was the hardest thing Joe had ever done. The shock and anguish in his mother's voice hit him so hard it was all he could do to hold on to his last shred of self-control. He had to be strong for his mother, so he was. Barely.

"No!" she moaned. "Please, God, don't let my baby be gone."

He closed his eyes and leaned against the wall. "I can't believe it either."

"Are you sure, Joe? They make mistakes sometimes. They think they know it's one person, but it turns out to really be someone else."

"I'm sorry, Mom, I saw him myself." His chest tightened at the memory.

"What happened?"

"He was...he was stabbed."

She made a noise that reminded him of a needy kitten. "Did he, was it bad for him?"

At least he could be truthful about that part. "He died almost instantly."

"Do they have any idea who did this to him?"

"Not yet, but they're being very thorough."

"I hope they find the bastard."

"Me too, Mom." He closed his eyes and leaned harder against the wall.

"When are you coming home?"

"Not for a few days. There are some things I need to take care of here." He swallowed. "And I want to bring Justin back with me."

"Be careful, sweetheart." Her voice broke.

"I will, Mom. I promise."

They said their goodbyes and he clicked off his cell phone. He paced for a time, then dropped onto his brother's couch and glared down at the papers strewn across the coffee table. He reached for his coffee cup, grimaced at the lukewarm liquid, and sat it back down.

The papers included a journal with times, dates, reconstructed conversations, and personal details that shook Joe to his toes. Justin had done his job, and done it well. It had taken some serious digging to gather this much information. Enough digging to make somebody suspicious.

The clippings and printouts surprised and worried him the most. Justin had been convinced a conspiracy existed against some group he called "V," whatever that meant. The clippings from newspapers as far-flung as Florida, California, New York, *The Chronicle Herald* across the border in Nova Scotia—even Japan and Russia—were articles or personal ads that meant nothing to him, but he sensed a pattern. The printouts were from several different emails. How his brother got access to them was a mystery, but the messages were to and from members of an organization called the "Alliance of True Humanity," and spouted hatred and fear toward a group they called "vampires" claiming this group's goal was destruction of the human race. Was Justin's "V" group the same as this "vampire" group?

Joe contemplated the word. It reminded him of every Saturday late movie. "So maybe these 'vampires' are just plain old human. Maybe they just really suck." He laughed as he picked Justin's journal back up. He'd skimmed it, but hadn't read it. It seemed an invasion of privacy to read the more personal details, but he wondered if he should.

It seemed to him that calling a group of people "not quite human," was simple racism. But in his journal, his brother had used those same words. Then, a few pages later, Justin admitted he was involved with one of them, this mysterious "C".

"They call themselves vampire," Justin had written. "I don't care what they call themselves, or what other people think they are. They seem very human to me, and I love C. with all my heart."

Joe pulled out his laptop. His brother's, he was sure, had been taken by the police when they searched Justin's home. A quick search told him what he'd suspected. The word "vampire" was loaded, for sure.

Chapter 3

Veronica was preparing to extract a second piece of DNA from a previously tested sample. She suspected contamination with foreign DNA, so a second test was necessary. A presence appeared behind her. She twisted, her body on high alert and ready for an attack.

"Doctor Teal?"

The tall, lanky, middle-aged man was dressed entirely in black, his expression blank except for the intelligent, questioning eyes. She had the feeling he knew everything that went on around him—even inside her head. There was no perceptible brush against her mind, but she was positive he had been in her thoughts.

"May I help you?"

"Could we speak in private?"

She stored the sample, pulled off her latex gloves, and motioned toward her office. Once inside the glass-enclosed room, she closed the door and propped one hip on her desk. The Guardian made her nervous, and she hated that feeling. She had done her job and turned in the reports from the murder site. "Is there a problem?"

"I just wanted to go over your findings with you."

A wave of heat blew through Veronica. "I assure you, my findings are accurate. A vampire, whose DNA profile I included in my report, killed the human approximately six hours before the body was discovered."

"Actually, we were curious about *why* you included the time of death and the DNA profile. We would understand if you needed the profile to distinguish between human and vampire, but there seemed to be no question about that. There rarely is."

Suspicion that the conversation had turned in an unwelcome direction had her clenching her hands. "I thought the timing and DNA profile might help you identify the killer."

A miniscule smile pulled at the Guardian's lips. "I suspected as much. Dr. Teal, you need to understand your role as consultant. While I appreciate your desire to be thorough, in a case such as this one, your job is to let us know—as quickly as possible—if one of our kind is involved. If we require anything else, we will let you know. DNA, even as rapid as our processes are, wastes time."

Icy cold realization skittered through her body. "You won't even try to find the killer, will you?"

"Why should we?"

She could barely speak her jaw was so tight. "Because killing humans is illegal among our kind. Besides, it's the right thing to do?"

Never had she heard a laugh so cold and harsh. "The 'right thing' is a very subjective term. The death of a human is rarely important to the vampire, and this one appears to be insignificant and unlikely to cause repercussions."

"I see."

He studied her for a moment. "Perhaps you are not clear on the role of the Guardians."

"You protect us."

"Yes, protect the *vampire*. We aren't in the

business of protecting humans, except as it concerns our own needs."

The icy feeling spread to her arms. "Humans aren't important."

"Of course they are. We couldn't survive without them." With that, the Guardian turned and walked out her office door.

An image of the handsome man lying discarded and bloody on the hard, cold, slippery rocks filled her mind. The human police had no hope of catching the killer, and even if they did, the Guardians would never let one of the vampire be prosecuted by humans. Bottom line: this human victim and his family would never see justice done.

Shoving her feelings aside, she headed back to her workstation. Was it possible she had too much sympathy for an inferior species? Then again, maybe human and vampire were not as different as everyone thought.

***

Joe's lightweight jacket did little to protect him against the chilly evening breeze as he walked along the shoreline behind Ned's Lobster Shack and the Seafood Market. The Coast Guard station was nearby, so he could watch as their boats pulled from the dock and headed out. He wondered if his brother had spent much time here. He hoped so, the sound of the waves against the rocks soothed and exhilarated at the same time.

"Mr. Sullivan," The female voice came through his cell. "I'm sorry to keep you on hold for so long, especially since we played phone tag all day. What can I do for you?"

He tried to swallow back his trepidation. "Thank

you for speaking with me, Dr. Hutchins. I was hoping you could tell me if you've performed the autopsy yet."

"We'll be doing that first thing tomorrow. I should be able to release the body for burial before the end of the week."

It was horrible, the thought of burying his brother, but that wasn't his main concern right now. "Did you find anything useful on your initial exam?"

"Sir, I can't discuss ongoing investigations."

Something in her voice sent a cold chill through him. "How long did my brother lay on that beach?"

"Look, I'd like to help you, but—"

"You can't discuss an ongoing investigation."

"I'm truly sorry."

"Thanks anyway." He clicked off the phone and fought the urge to hurl it hard out over the rocks into the deep, cold, unyielding ocean. Maybe he'd been reading his brother's conspiracy theories too long, but something didn't feel right.

"You must be Joe," a voice said.

He spun to confront the man standing within arm's length of him. He'd been so lost in thought he hadn't heard anybody approach. "Yeah, I'm Joe. Who are you?"

"My name is Conner. I was a friend of your brother." The man closed his eyes for a moment, while sheer agony crossed his face. "I can't believe he's dead."

Joe studied the man wearing jeans and a black jacket, his red hair a little ruffled in the cold breeze coming from the bay. He seemed honestly to be mourning his brother's death, but was that for real? Was this C, or was this Justin's murderer? Or were they one and the same? He decided to focus on the obvious. "How well did you know my brother?"

Conner seemed to hesitate, looking away, then back. "We knew each other quite well."

He was a little younger than Joe's thirty-two. Soft-spoken, and good looking, he was just the type of man his brother would fall for. "Did you know what he was looking into?"

Conner's gaze shot left, then right, then back to Joe. "The Alliance of True Humanity. Yes, I did."

"So you know about these inhuman beings?"

Conner winced. "The vampires, yes."

Joe studied the man. Justin's journal claimed C was one of the creatures, but there was nothing he could see that pointed to Conner being anything but human? Then again, would he be able to tell? Just how weird were these things?

"Not that different. Not really."

Joe took a reflexive step back. "How did you know what I was thinking?"

Conner swallowed, straightened his back slightly, and met Joe's gaze. "Because you projected the thought, and we vampires have strong psychic ability."

"Well, shit."

****

The predator lurked in the pre-dawn darkness of Lobster Cove. There were plenty of places along the edges of this tiny town where the streetlights didn't reach. He'd stumbled onto the perfect place to practice his trade. Dressed completely in black, with the hood of his jacket pulled down low, he blended with the shadows. His eyes, used to the dimness, easily caught sight of his prey.

He smiled.

The slim blonde moved with confidence through the dim light of a crescent moon, then all but vanished in the gloom of shadow. Again and again, like one of those old silent movies his last foster dad was so crazy about. That guy was one of the better dads, and living with the man and his sweet wife hadn't been horrible or anything. He'd left because they were pretty strict about behavior, and he wanted to be free to do as he pleased.

He moved closer, silently stalking his prey. Slipping from shadow to darker shadow, elation tingled through his chest at how easy this would be. No woman who didn't belong in his world should be walking alone an hour before dawn.

She must be a tourist. Probably had a wad of green in that shoulder bag that she wasn't even trying to hold close to her. Smiling, sixteen-year-old Kevin Sanders moved in. Rushing at the woman, he grabbed for her bag.

All he got was a fist full of nothing.

Shaken, Kevin looked around for his target—who was watching him from about two feet to his left. Weird, but just a little glitch in his plan.

He lunged toward his victim again, pulling out his knife as he went. "Just hand me the bag and nobody will get hurt."

She stood there, not moving, not running. The best he could tell in the dim light, she didn't even look scared. Maybe she had something wrong with her. That should make life even easier for him.

He walked right up to her, waving the knife a little, just to show her who was boss. "Hand over your money."

The blonde smiled and he got an odd feeling in his gut, a feeling that something was off, but he ignored the warning. How could something this simple go wrong?

"You need to go home," she said.

He laughed. This idiot was probably one of those crusaders who seemed to think all they had to do was throw money around and be nice to the "poor, misguided kids." He'd show her who was misguided. "Hand it over, bitch, or I'll make you wish you had."

"Can't say I didn't warn you."

She looked into his eyes, and his gut twisted. The bitch had eyes like nothing he'd ever seen, eyes of a color that couldn't be natural on human or animal, eyes that pulled him in.

Eyes of a predator.

Her hand touched his shoulder. When had she got close enough to touch him? *Go*, his head insisted. His feet refused.

His sleeve was shoved up, and a sharp pain shot through his left forearm, sort of like the stab when the doctor takes blood. His reflex was to jerk away from the pain, but he couldn't make his body cooperate. He tried to turn his head to see, but found he couldn't. He strained his eyes to the side. Damn, he had to know what was happening to him.

Finally, he managed to catch a glimpse of golden hair draped over his arm. It took him a minute to figure out she sucked on his wrist.

She looked up at him and smiled. A drop of blood ran out one side of her mouth and she stuck out her tongue to pull it back in. His mind refused to believe what his eyes told him, that the crazy blonde was drinking his blood like a freaking vampire.

This wasn't happening. No freaking way. But he could feel the pull of her mouth on his arm. Shit! This was like a damn horror novel, or a nightmare like the ones he used to have when he was little.

Yeah that was it. Nightmare. That made a lot of sense.

He closed his eyes and waited. He could still feel the suction of the bitch's mouth on his arm. Something about what she was doing sent spikes of desire through him, which was seriously freaky. Not that it mattered. All that mattered was escaping from this lunatic.

He tried again to pull away, but couldn't make anything move except his eyes. He couldn't even open his mouth to scream. For the first time in his life, he would love to see a stupid cop. Then again, he wasn't sure even a gun would stop this bitch.

Crazy Blonde licked his arm where she'd sucked on him. His stomach lurched, and he swallowed hard. He told himself he was a man, and men didn't puke on women, even crazy ones.

Then her gaze caught his. Her eyes looked almost black, and he could have sworn she was poking around in his brain. That was crazy, right?

"You are going home," she said. "You will feel a need to do something more with your life. You want to go to school and get a job and show everybody that you are important. You'll stop stealing for a living, and you won't remember any of this." She smiled as she turned and strolled away.

Slowly his body once again became his own, and he headed toward home. One thing he knew, he'd never forget tonight.

****

Veronica was almost to her apartment when she allowed herself to let go of the lingering annoyance from the episode with that would-be criminal. The human was still a child, and she was rather sorry for him. She hoped the fear she'd made sure he'd experienced and the desire for a better life she'd planted would push him toward doing something more with his life than running around in the middle of the night looking for people to steal from. Most vampires thought of humans as nothing more than a source of the blood her kind needed to survive, but she couldn't keep from seeing them as cousins.

From that thought came one of irritation with the Guardians for their uncaring attitude toward humans. Maybe the difference was that she was a biochemist specializing in genetic differences in species, and understanding the difference between the two species was a long-time interest of hers. She knew and understood the physiological and genetic gulf between vampire and human, and it wasn't nearly as wide as her kind would like to believe.

Before she had time to think about it anymore, she pulled out her cell phone and dialed. "Hello, Pat. You're up early."

"And you're up late,"

"I'm just getting off work, and I wanted to check in with you."

"I take it you want to know about the murder," Pat said. "Name is Justin Sullivan. He was killed by exsanguination due to having his throat cut—like that wasn't obvious from the scene. What you probably don't know is that the crime scene techs tested the soil and the rocks, and they can't account for the amount of blood that was lost from the victim. We found no evidence that the body was moved, however."

Veronica sighed. "Anything that might indicate who the murderer was?"

"No, but you knew that was a long shot."

"Sometimes long shots do pay off."

"Not this time. I'll let you know if anything changes."

"I'd appreciate it, Pat."

"No problem. I'd really like to see the creep who did this pay, and I have a pretty good idea you're the best hope of that happening."

"Thanks for having faith in me."

"You understand what happened, I only have guidelines to follow, and a vague idea of why I'm supposed to call you."

"I'll do what I can, but you understand I'm just a glorified crime scene tech, Right?"

"Nonetheless, you're in the loop, and I'm not."

Veronica winced. "I'll see what I can do."

They hung up, and Veronica went to her apartment considering that if she was the best hope of bringing the culprit to justice, there wasn't much hope at all.

****

Joe sauntered into the Bar Harbor Sheriff's Office trying hard to look like he belonged. A young man in uniform sat at the front desk, typing two-fingered on a computer keyboard. He looked up and his eyes widened. "Holy crap!"

Joe walked over to the officer and held out his hand. "Hello, I'm Joe Sullivan."

The officer slowly reached out to shake his hand. "You look just like—" His Adam's apple moved up and down, and he shifted in his seat. "I'm sorry."

Joe nodded. "Justin was my twin. Actually, that's why I'm here. I'm hoping to find out how the investigation is going."

"I'm sorry. the sheriff isn't in right now."

"That's too bad. I'd hoped to talk to him." Joe had waited to go in until the sheriff went to lunch. Luckily, when the sheriff left, so did several of the staff. He figured he might have a better chance of getting information from someone other than the head lawman, and the fewer people around the better.

"I'm sorry," the officer repeated.

He sighed. "I'm sure he stays busy."

"Yeah, he does."

"You know, I just realized, you probably don't have a lot of murders around here. I'll bet your sheriff is pretty stressed out about now."

"Yes, he is." The officer narrowed his eyes. "But he'll get the guy. He always does."

"I'm sure he will. In fact, I'll bet he already has a bunch of clues."

The officer, the name on his uniform was Woods, looked distinctly uncomfortable. "Well, I'm not exactly involved in the murder investigation."

"Damn, I really would like to know something. It's rough to lose a brother, especially a twin brother." Joe let his sadness and frustration show. "You understand, don't you, Officer Woods?"

Woods nodded. "I'm sure it's hard."

"Just knowing something's being done would help. I just want to know the sheriff is making some headway toward catching my twin's murderer."

"The sheriff's a good man, as are the detectives

and state police working the case."

Joe sighed and rubbed a hand over his face. "Mom's a basket case. If I could just assure her the authorities have some lead. Anything."

The young officer shifted in his chair. "I do hear things." He looked around as if making sure no one was listening before leaning across the desk toward Joe. "I've heard they didn't find any useful evidence at the site. No footprints, no drag marks, not even enough blood." He winced. "I probably shouldn't have said that."

Joe's stomach turned, but he made himself smile. "It's okay, I'm a scientist." Biology teacher at a small college actually, but this guy didn't need to know that. "I know it sounds kinda weird, it being my brother and all, but I can't help being curious. What do you mean not enough blood?"

"Are you sure, Mr. Sullivan? It doesn't seem appropriate."

"Call me Joe, please. Now you've got me wondering. Do me a favor and don't make me lay awake at night worrying."

The young man swallowed hard. "That wouldn't be right. Especially since it was me who screwed up." He glanced around again, then leaned toward Joe. "There was more blood missing from him than could be accounted for at the scene. He must have been moved, but the crime scene folks didn't find any evidence to suggest how that had been done."

"Thank you, Officer. I appreciate your help."

"I'm sorry about your brother."

"Thank you." He stood and shook the young man's hand. Then headed for the door before he got the nice officer in trouble.

Once outside, reality smacked him in the head. So the police knew very little. Figures. Would a tourist town's sheriff's department have the means to solve a crime like this one? Even if the state police was involved, they still had only the evidence to work with—and apparently they hadn't found much of that.

What about the FBI? What was a Federal "consultant" doing at a local crime scene? A scientist, of all things. What was that about?

Then there was the big question, did Justin's death have anything to do with his conspiracy theory? Up until now, Joe had been able to convince himself his brother's investigation and death were not related.

Even if a conspiracy of some sort did exist, it was likely a loose organization headed by a couple of people with grandiose delusions. It was hard to believe that any group of the magnitude Justin feared could be real.

Like the non-human people. This Conner didn't seem like some weird creature. Maybe he was ill and his delusions had spread to Justin. Maybe he hadn't "read his mind". Maybe he'd guessed what Joe was thinking.

Then again, something he'd seen in Justin's journal kept pushing into his mind. About how the not-quite-humans needed to drink human blood to survive. That couldn't be what happened to the rest of Justin's blood. Could it?

****

"All right, girl. Are you going to tell me what's got you all twitchy, or do I have to beat it out of you?" Tim acted out the "twitchy" part with a wiggle straight from one of his drag queen acts.

Veronica eyed her friend. "Twitchy, huh?"

"Very much twitchy." He sat on her couch and patted the seat beside him. "Come here and tell momma all about it."

"You're a creepy man, you know that?"

"Why thank you, dear. How sweet you are to point that out."

She sat with one foot under her, facing Tim. "I love your way with sarcasm."

"Just one of the many services I offer."

"You got that from a T-shirt."

"No, the T-shirt got it from me."

Laughing, she put her hand on his arm. "I don't know what I'd do without you."

The humor dropped from his expression. "Even if I *am* human?"

Tears unexpectedly filled her eyes, and she looked away so Tim wouldn't see. "You're my closest friend. That's all that matters."

"Hey." He slid closer and stroked her hair. "I'm here for you, girlfriend, even if you are a bloodsucker."

Veronica laughed in spite of herself. "Thanks. I appreciate that. I think."

"You'd be in big trouble if they found out how much you've told me, wouldn't you?"

"Yes, I guess I would. The Guardians don't like humans to know we exist." She stood and wandered over to the window that looked out over the woody area and toward the town. "Damn Guardians."

"Whoa." She heard Tim come up behind her. "What's got you so pissed at these Guardian folks?"

She put her head down, wondering if she should

dig herself in deeper than she already had. She needed to talk, to let out some of the anger and worry that she kept buried deep inside. The unvoiced emotions festered like a wound when a splinter gets left inside, swelling with every passing day, painfully stretching her nerves almost beyond their limit. If she didn't release the pressure soon, all the crap she'd trapped inside her was likely to spew out like a geyser.

Turning she reached out to take Tim's hand in hers. "A man was killed, and they don't care because he's human."

He tightened his grip on her hand. "We humans have been doing a reasonable job of taking care of ourselves for a while now." He shrugged. "So they don't care. Big deal. We can take care of our own."

"Not against us you can't."

Tim's eyes widened as he drew in a long, slow breath. "This guy was killed by one of your people?"

She nodded. "Yes, he was killed by a vampire. The Guardians don't care, and humans are unlikely to find the one responsible."

"What would happen if our police did find the bastard?"

"Human police couldn't capture him. If by some miracle they did, the Guardians wouldn't dare leave him in human custody."

"That's what I figured. So what can we do?"

Veronica stared at Tim. "*We?*"

"Well sure." He put his back to her and held out his hands in a gun-aiming stance. "We can be *Charlie's Angels*."

Laughter bubbled up from her chest. "Who will be Charlie?"

Tim made a waving gesture. "We don't need no stinking man to tell us what to do. How about we be *Starsky and Hutch*? You can be Hutch, since you got the blonde hair. I'll be Starsky."

She faced Tim and took his hands in hers. "I truly appreciate you being there for me, but I don't want you involved in something that might get sticky."

"Oh honey, Sticky is my middle name."

Confused, she studied his face. Was he making a joke? "Your middle name is James."

He laughed. "My sweet, literal Veronica."

His cell phone chirped and he turned away to pull it out. His voice dropped two octaves when he answered. "Yes?" There was silence for a moment, then, "Not again! I'm on my way."

"Something wrong?"

"The client from hell just got arrested. Again." He sighed. "I'll be checking back with you. Don't you dare go off on any adventures without me."

"No adventures, Sticky. I'll remember."

He grinned as he kissed her on the forehead, then headed out the door.

Adventure? That's not what she'd call what she was considering. Unwise, unheard of, or just plain stupid. Yeah, that might describe it. Nobody messes with the Guardians. Nobody. Not if they knew even a little about the formidable protectors of the vampire species.

Maybe the best way to describe what she was about to do would be suicidal.

Chapter 4

Joe listened to the rhythmic crashing of the waves against the wooden poles holding up the public pier he stood on the edge of. He hoped the sound might help calm his nerves. Maybe it did, a little, but he still thought he might jump out of his skin at any time. As darkness fell, the fog thickened to the point he could no longer see the ocean even from this close. Only the echoing rhythm told him he stood near the vast and powerful force of water.

"Joe."

He jerked around so fast he almost tripped over his own feet. "How did you do that? I was listening for you, damn it!"

Conner stepped closer to him. "My kind can move faster and more quietly than yours."

"Wanna tell me what else 'your kind' can do?"

"Not at the moment."

Joe's stomach tightened at the words. "Why do I get the feeling you guys don't like talking about yourselves?"

"You must understand, we have had to keep ourselves hidden from humans for thousands of years."

For a moment, he couldn't breathe. "Thousands?" he forced out.

Conner nodded. "Yes."

"Is it true you are dependent on us to survive?"

"Yes. We must drink a small amount of human blood or suffer from severe anemia."

"Small amount? Like when a shark only takes an arm or leg?"

"No. Only a few ounces." The man, or whatever he was, took a step toward Joe. "Please, I can only stay here a few minutes, and I have things to tell you."

"Can't be seen with a human?"

Conner looked away a moment. When he turned back, he met Joe's gaze and held it. "My being with you puts both of us in danger."

The truth of the statement hit Joe right in the belly. "Sorry, I guess I'm a little oversensitive right now."

Conner's hand gripped his shoulder. "I understand. Your brother was a brave and moral man and I shall miss him. Still, my feelings likely fade in comparison to yours."

Hearing his brother described that way stung his eyes and filled his throat with barely held-back grief. "He was a good person."

"Yes, and he wanted badly to help defeat the gathering evil in our midst."

Joe forced his focus back to what was important. "The conspiracy."

"I believe Justin was making headway into the heart of the evil. As a human, he could get answers none of us could."

"No vampires could, you mean."

Conner looked out into the sea. "We prefer not to use that term with humans, because of the connotations your kind have added to the original meaning."

"Whatever you call yourselves, how do I know these 'evil' folks aren't actually the good guys?"

"Honestly, I'm not sure how I can prove anything to you. You said you had Justin's journal. Look at what he believed, that likely will be the only way to sway you."

The vampire looked around while shifting foot to foot. Joe realized he needed to put aside his misgivings long enough to listen. To pay attention to what this man had to say. "Okay, what is it you want to tell me?"

Conner glanced around again, then stepped closer. "As I was saying, I believe Justin was making inroads into those who want to destroy the vampire species. As his brother, and presumably a person with access to that information, I believe you may be in grave danger."

Whatever else he might be, this guy was serious—and so was the situation. "I'm still sorting out the details," Joe said, "but so far I've only seen general information. I haven't founds names, or specific locations, or plans, or anything else that could be useful."

Conner took a deep breath and slowly blew it out. "The last time I spoke to Justin he told me he had important information. We were meeting for a late dinner that night, he said he had to check something out first, but he never showed up. I was terrified, and unfortunately, my fears were correct."

Joe's breath caught and shivers rushed up his spine. "I haven't found anything like that."

"I'm sure any such information would be well hidden." Conner shot a glance around him and leaned toward Joe. "Either he really did know something important, or somebody thought he did."

"Or he wouldn't be dead." Joe swallowed hard.

"I should go now. Please be careful." Conner

touched his arm, real concern evident in his eyes. "Whoever killed Justin doesn't know what you have or have not discovered. I don't want you to be hurt."

"Thank you."

Conner nodded before he disappeared into the thick fog. Joe turned and followed, listening as he walked for anything that might indicate someone was near. As he headed toward Justin's apartment, he admitted to himself Conner's words had spooked him. The man truly seemed to have cared for his brother and his concern for Joe seemed genuine.

He was unlocking the apartment door when he remembered what his brother's notes said. For that matter, Conner himself had admitted vampires were strong psychics. Had he just been manipulated?

Lying awake most of the long night, he wondered just what kind of mess his twin had wandered into. Had Justin trusted the wrong person? Was Conner even "C"? How could Joe know who to trust, especially when beings existed who were indistinguishable from humans, and had the ability to skew a person's reality to suit their own agenda?

He had to find some answers. And he thought he knew just where to start.

****

Veronica eyed her co-worker with irritation. He'd followed her into the employee parking lot, and the scent of desire came off him with enough strength to make her want to run in the other direction.

Not that Todd Kennedy wasn't a good-looking man. In truth, he was quite handsome, she just wasn't interested in mating—either casually or long-term. Aware her lack of interest was unusual, she was inclined to try to stay away from confrontation. Still, if the guy pushed it, she wasn't above letting him know, in no uncertain terms, that she wasn't interested.

As she approached her car, the man walked faster until he trotted. Without looking his way, she climbed into her Lexus and pulled smoothly out of the space and toward the road. She easily blocked his anger with her mental shields, but out her rearview mirror, she saw the anger on his face, and her own smile as she considered his arrogance. She would choose her own sexual companions, and bullying only irritated her.

Ten minutes later, she parked her car on the street outside her building and sat pondering the invisible waves of emotion swirling around her. The waves were so strong, the edges touched her before she turned onto her street, and curiosity was firing hard inside her. A human, someone with a strong emotional force, was nearby. That wasn't unusual. Humans tended to have strong emotions and project them without even knowing. This human, though, projected strength and focus she'd never sensed from a human. Odd, and somehow exciting.

She opened the door and slid out of her car, feeling the mental strength increase. Amazing. Her breath drew in hard and long. The human behind her had serious psychic ability, though she doubted he or she was aware of it. After making sure her shields were in place, she turned to discover who this gifted human was.

"I know you're there, you might as well come on out."

When the man stepped toward her, her breath caught in her chest. Even having met him, spoken to him, knowing the victim was his brother, even then it was like seeing a dead man standing before her. A heart-stoppingly handsome dead man.

"You wouldn't be much of an FBI agent if you didn't know," he said.

She bit back the threatening smile. "As I told you before, I'm only a consultant."

"Who spends her nights in the basement of the Old Seabird Mansion."

She crossed her arms across her chest and glared at him. "And you know this how?"

He smiled. "You really aren't an agent, are you? I've been keeping an eye on you."

Anger sputtered, but wouldn't flare, probably because she was too intrigued by this guy. "The old Seabird Mansion is where I work."

"It's a beautiful place, I'll give you that. Queen Anne, I believe, complete with tower. But you don't work inside the main house. You work in a basement. At night. Sounds shady to me."

"Ha-ha." Heat rose through Veronica as her jaw clenched, and her hands fisted. "I'm a biochemist and my lab is below the house."

He raised one dark eyebrow. "Interesting place to put a laboratory."

She bit her lip to keep from kissing—no that wasn't right—to keep from hitting what-ever-the-hell his name was. Her gaze caught on his mouth and held. Full, luscious lips. She wanted badly to taste them.

"Joe."

Her attention jerked to his eyes. "What?"

"You asked what my name was, it's Joe. Joe Sullivan."

Had she asked him his name? She remembered

wondering, but she hadn't asked him. Had she? She didn't think so, but she must have.

"What's your name, Dr. FBI?"

"Veronica Teal."

"Named for Veronica Mars, or the old comic book Veronica?"

She met his gaze with a hard, steady glare. "Neither. I was named for Veronica Lake."

"The movie star?"

"You've heard of her?"

He shrugged. "My grandmother is a huge fan of classic movies."

"Dad's an old film buff." Not exactly, but she wasn't about to admit her father had an affair with Ms. Lake—in 1942—and had never lost his fascination for the human.

"Who had an affair?"

"What are you talking about?"

He held up his hands as if in surrender. "Hey, you were the one saying something about an affair. In nineteen forty-something, I believe."

Okay, enough of this. "I didn't say anything."

He leaned toward her, his nose almost touching hers. "I damn well heard you."

"Well, you must have imagined it, because I didn't say anything about an affair."

Great, the woman's loony tunes, she heard him say.

"Me? You're the one who's hearing things." she pointed out.

Joe blinked and took two steps back.

I didn't say that out loud. I'm sure I didn't.

She heard, and irritation crawled up her spine. What game was he playing?

"You must have spoken. How else would I know?" The confusion in his eyes had her rethinking the situation. She mentally replayed the last few minutes, and a sharp realization stabbed her. "We can hear each other's thoughts."

Joe stared at her. "How can that be?"

"No idea." She focused on slamming down her strongest defenses against psychic invasion.

"You do know. This has happened to you before."

Not with a human!

She tried to block the errant thought.

Joe stepped back again, wide eyes locked on hers. "You're a vampire!" He gasped.

She opened her mouth to deny the idea, then realized it was a little late for hiding behind lies.

"Yes," she told him. "I am. How do you know about vampires?"

He looked at her for a long moment, then slowly shook his head. "I'm pretty sure I'm either in a really strange dream, or an episode of the *Twilight Zone*."

"You aren't the only one." The sky was beginning to lighten; she had to make a decision. Now. "Come with me, we'll talk."

"Can't tolerate the sunlight?"

His sarcastic tone made her want to scream. She would have liked to walk away, but knew she had to see this through or it would just get worse over time. "As a matter of fact, I'm highly sensitive to the sun."

She turned toward her building, and Joe fell into step behind her.

His thoughts reached out to her. He hoped he didn't live to regret trusting her. Unless she killed him and drained his blood.

"Oh good grief, don't be so melodramatic." She sighed as she turned the key in the lock and ushered him into her lair.

Chapter 5

Joe followed Veronica into a perfectly normal looking, nineteenth-century home that had been converted into apartments. The yellow, well-cared for building was gorgeous. And so was the woman.

In fact, Veronica was probably the most beautiful woman he had ever seen, which had him wondering how many of the "beautiful people" weren't people at all.

They walked into an open lobby, with an oak staircase leading to the second floor. Two doors, with apartment numbers on them, led off the lobby. Joe was looking for the basement door, when he realized she was heading up the stairs.

She opened the door and waved him into a normal apartment, including windows allowing the morning sun to touch the classic couch, chair, coffee table, and three smaller tables scattered around the room.

"Have a seat," she said. "Would you like something to drink?"

"What would you suggest, Blood Lite, maybe?"

"I was thinking coffee, or maybe orange juice. I do have wine if you'd like that, though it is a little early in the day."

"If you're making coffee, that would be great."

"I am." She turned and headed toward the back of the apartment.

He paced for a few minutes while he mentally kicked his own butt. He was upset and frustrated. That was why he'd been sarcastic. He looked out one of the two windows. The sunlight gave the room a cheery feel. The apartment was decorated nicely. A soft green couch with yellow pillows sat on one side. Simple decorations on the walls and coffee table. A small round table with a vase of some sort of flowers sat by the front window. Feminine, but not in-your-face girly. Soft but practical. Warm.

Wait a minute. She said she couldn't tolerate the sun. She'd had to get inside to avoid it, but the windows allowed the daylight to come right into her home. What the hell?

Curious, he inspected the glass and frame to see if he could detect something special about them. If not, he'd just been conned. This close, he could see something unusual about the light falling on his hands and the table in front of the window. He had a suspicion that some of the wavelengths were either missing or altered.

After a bit more inspection, a brownish substance gathered in one corner of the frame caught his eye. It only took a moment to realize the window was coated with some substance. The stuff must block whatever hurt the bloodsuckers.

He sat on the overstuffed green couch, dropped his head into his hands, and got back to the berating of himself. Being a jerk to this woman wouldn't help anything. She couldn't help what she was any more than he could.

Veronica plopped two full cups onto the coffee table. "That was rather insulting."

Joe looked at the gorgeous woman standing in front of him, fists on her hips, eyes flashing in anger. "Well, stop listening to my thoughts and you won't be insulted."

"I didn't—" She closed her eyes for a moment, then dropped onto the couch beside him. "This isn't possible."

"Don't like this connecting with a human thing?"

"It shouldn't be happening—and not just because you're human."

He picked up his coffee and took a sip, and she cringed.

"I'm sorry. I was coming out here to ask what you take in your coffee."

"I prefer black." He couldn't resist reaching out to touch the silky blonde hair that flowed down her back all the way to her perfectly shaped ass. He could get lost just looking at her. What would it be like to hold her close, to kiss her until she melted in his arms? To touch her, taste her, feel her beneath him?

She shot to her feet and backed away from him. "What are you thinking?"

He shrugged. "I'm thinking about the beautiful woman beside me."

Her hand was trembling as she put it over her heart. "But I'm vampire and you're—"

"A man." He rose to his feet and went to her. Her gorgeous sea green eyes widened, but she stood waiting for him.

He slid one hand under her hair, the other around her waist, then nudged her toward him. Sure she'd resist, he was shocked when she leaned against him.

His lips touched her warm, firm, perfect mouth,

and he heard himself groan. Then her arms wrapped around his neck, and a soft sigh shot heat straight to his loins.

She leaned into him, and her soft curves fit against him in all the right places. His body hardened, while his thinking processes blurred. He had to have this woman. he had to be inside her. He needed her as much as he needed his next breath.

All at once an image of Justin lying cold and dead on the rocky shoreline rushed into his mind. He shoved Veronica away.

"Joe?"

"Sorry," he muttered as he all but ran for the door and down the stairs. He didn't stop until he couldn't breathe anymore and was forced to lean against a tree and allow oxygen back into his lungs. "What the hell is wrong with me?"

A passer-by gave him a wary look, turned, and dashed across the street.

He ignored the guy and went back to berating himself. His brother was in the morgue and he was getting it on with some kind of creature that looked, felt, and tasted like a human woman, but wasn't. Hell, she might have orchestrated that whole seduction scene to keep him from doing what he'd intended to do—try to get info from her.

He had no idea just what these vampire beings were capable of, and he'd be smart to be wary of all of them. If he could figure out who was what.

Sighing, he realized he needed some distance and time to think. As soon as he got back to Justin's apartment building, he got in his rental car and headed out of town.

****

Veronica smiled at the name that popped up on her cell phone. "Hello, Ethan. Thanks for returning my call."

"No problem. So what's up?"

Anxiety twisted her belly. What was she doing? Admitting anything about these strange feelings could cause her serious headaches.

"Veronica, are you all right?"

She was being silly. This was Ethan, an old friend and an anthropologist. If anybody would accept what she said without judging, it was him. So she swallowed back her fear.

"I'm fine, but I would like to discuss something with you if you have a few minutes."

"What's on your mind?"

"I um…you work with humans, are fascinated with their cultures. So I thought you might have some insight for me."

"Insight into what?"

"Have you ever…ever heard…?"

A low chuckle came through the cell phone. "Spit it out, Teal."

She sighed. "Fine. Have you ever been attracted to a human?"

"As in sexually attracted?"

"Yes." This was a mistake. What was she thinking?

"Actually, yes. I have."

She actually felt her jaw drop. "Could you be more specific?"

"Just what you said, there have been times when I was sexually attracted to a human woman."

She bit her lip, then took hold of her fear and

continued. "Have you ever, well, acted on your attraction?"

"As in sex with a human?"

"No!" She swallowed. "Just maybe…kissing the human."

His laugh had her face going hot. "Yes, I have. A fellow professor, actually, who was very nice. We talked a lot. One day we found ourselves face to face and we kissed. That was all that happened. She took a job in Wyoming soon after that. We still email from time to time."

"So, kissing's not so terrible."

"Want to tell me about this human you're attracted to?"

She considered not saying anything, but she knew Ethan wouldn't stop until he got the information out of her. "A human was killed, the coroner called me. The brother of the victim saw me at the scene, heard me use my FBI cover, and he's been following me. He seems to think I can help him figure out who killed his brother."

"Can you?"

"I don't know, but it wouldn't matter if I did. It was one of us."

"I figured you would say that. So what did you tell him?"

"That I couldn't help him. But he won't give up."

"So, he's following you around like a puppy, and you have the hots for him, as my students say?"

"No, he's serious about getting answers and I can't blame him. He was outside my apartment building this morning, and I invited him up. Seemed preferable to frying in the sun."

"You invited him into your apartment?"

She swallowed. "He knows what we are, Ethan."

"How did he find out?"

"No idea, but figured out I'm vampire. And we can hear each other's thoughts. And he kissed me." She closed her eyes and waited for his reaction.

"Wait a minute, he can read your mind?"

"No, not exactly. We were hearing each other's thoughts. Like talking, but mental. Freaked both of us out."

"You freaked him out, so he kissed you?" Ethan's chuckle made her want to go to Tennessee just so she could smack his head.

"No. We talked for a while. The kiss just happened. Then he went tearing out of my apartment. Apparently kissing a vampire didn't appeal to him."

"Maybe you were just too much for the poor guy."

She closed her eyes and groaned. "Ethan."

He chuckled. Again. "Relax. So you and a human are attracted to each other. You're a grown woman. A gorgeous woman. Any straight man in his right mind— vampire or human—would be attracted to you."

She smiled in spite of herself. "You aren't, are you?"

He laughed. "Nobody ever said I was in my right mind. After all, I teach humans about human culture. Not to mention going on digs and sitting in the sun for long hours. Ask Spencer, he'll tell you the sun fried my brain a long time ago."

She licked her lips. "So you don't think that kiss was a big deal."

"Veronica, you know how I feel. I believe humans and vampires are not that different. Attraction is perfectly understandable."

"As long as nobody finds out."

A long sigh came through the phone. "I wouldn't presume to tell you what to do, but I do think it's prudent to be cautious. Vampires by nature are slightly paranoid and unyielding in their beliefs."

"Duly noted. Thanks for taking time to listen to my babbling, Dr. Drake."

"Veronica, be careful, okay?"

"I will, Ethan."

They said their goodbyes, and she sat back to contemplate the complexity of navigating the human world. Especially when one of those humans ignited heat in ways she hadn't imagined possible.

****

Kevin stared at the man getting into a car with a rental sticker on the back bumper. The man cranked the engine and drove away like the devil himself was after him. Either the guy in that car was the reporter Vincent said was dead, or he had a double. Like a doppelganger in one of the horror novels he didn't admit to reading. No sense asking to be teased.

He watched the car head away from town, and wondered what the truth really was. It didn't make sense. Not only had Vincent said the nosy reporter guy was dead, the murder had been reported on the local news.

Kevin's first instinct was to go find Vincent and tell him what he'd seen. Then it occurred to him that he probably wouldn't be believed. The whole bunch of guys who hung with Vince thought Kevin was a worthless kid as it was. If he showed up telling a crazy story, they'd probably just laugh.

Then again, if he played his cards right, the situation might offer an opportunity to prove his worth and loyalty to the organization. He might be young, but he was smart and strong. He'd come to Lobster Cove because that was where the action was, and he was tired of being a nothing. He wanted a chance to prove himself, to take his rightful place as a true, full member of the Alliance of True Humanity.

He might have just found that opportunity.

****

Velvet darkness was broken only by the light from the windows of houses covered the southwest corner of Lobster Cove as Veronica walked toward her job. To get to the lab, she had to go down Pine Avenue and turn right onto Second Street. Well, actually, she could go through the woods and save herself a lot of walk, but distance didn't bother her, and she liked seeing the tree lined streets of Lobster Cove. The people were nice too. The thought of humans sent her mind flipping right to the one who was stressing her out.

What the hell had happened that morning? A human male had thrown himself at her like he was starving and she was a...what...steak maybe? Worse, she'd thrown herself right back at him.

Forcing her thoughts to the present, she smiled at passers-by. It was quite chilly, so she was surprised so many humans were out. Then she caught a glimpse of a Lionel Lobster poster in a store window. The Harvest of the Sea Festival was coming up soon. Smiling, she headed out of the actual town area and into the fringe of forest. Here she was less likely to be observed, and could walk at a beyond-human-ability speed.

Less than two minutes later, she emerged from the

foliage near the restored mansion where her lab was located. She had only taken a couple of steps toward the back entrance, which led directly into the basement, when she sensed a strong psychic pull. Damn! Not again.

Turning, she met Joe's gaze through the shadowy darkness. "What do you want?"

He stepped toward her. "What I wanted this morning, but somehow never got around to asking. I want to ask for your help finding the person who killed my brother."

She put every bit of strength she had into holding her mental barriers closed to this human. "What makes you think I could, even if I wanted to?"

He took a half step closer, then stopped, as if he were as worried as she was about the odd link between them. "You're FBI."

She opened her mouth, only to be interrupted before she could say anything.

"Yeah, I know. You're only a consultant. Whatever the hell that means." He crossed his arms over his chest and glared her way. "Still, you must have connections. You can get answers. If you choose to."

She held his gaze. "And why would I want to help you?"

He lifted his chin and took two bold steps toward her. "Because you believe in justice."

"What makes you think…?" Obviously because he'd seen it in her mind. Damn.

"I'm not too happy with the situation either," he said. "Especially since you're the expert at this psychic thing. How do I know you aren't manipulating my thoughts?"

Veronica almost rolled her eyes like a frustrated middle-school girl. Instead, she sighed and gave him a narrow-eyed glare. "Yeah, I'd definitely manipulate you into…um, wanting me to help you solve your brother's murder."

The smug smile on his face had her clenching her teeth.

"So you didn't want me to kiss you this morning?"

"I want you to leave me alone."

"No you don't." He moved closer. "You enjoyed what we did."

"I didn't say I didn't."

He touched her arm, sending warm tingles through her entire body. "Help me find out what happened to Justin. Please."

His eyes were dark brown velvet, and they seemed to see right into her. She swallowed hard, forcing herself to focus on the situation and not the man. "Let the police handle it, Joe."

"Why don't you believe they'll catch the guy?"

Damn it all to hell! She increased her psychic boundaries, knowing full well it was a waste of energy. "Joe, it's crazy for an untrained person to go up against a murderer. Your brother is dead. I don't want you to be next."

"Then help me."

"I can't."

He stepped back, and his anger washed over her. "Can't or won't?"

"Joe…"

He turned and walked away. She watched him go until he disappeared into the shadows. When she again went toward the door to the lab, she went with a heavy feeling in the area of her heart. She understood, but there really wasn't anything she could do. Even if she could help him, getting involved in this case would anger the Guardians, and that was not something she had any intention of doing. Her career, her very life, could be ruined in a heartbeat.

A vision of Charlene lying cold and lifeless on that rocky beach flashed through her mind. As much as she wanted to strangle her sister sometimes, she loved her too. If this had happened to her, she would do everything in her power to see that the killer was brought to justice.

Then again, if it were a vampire that had been murdered, the Guardians would be looking for the killer.

Were humans so different, so less worthy, that they didn't deserve justice?

****

A restless night did nothing to calm his mind. The next afternoon Joe was still so angry and frustrated that he didn't pay attention to where he drove the country roads around Lobster Cove. The scenery was beautiful, but he barely noticed. When he finally went back into town and got his bearings, he was outside a bar called Murphy's.

Oh hell, why not?

He pushed open the heavy door and walked in.

The place was rustic, weathered boards for walls, plain dark wooden tables, basic wooden stools at the bar. The jukebox was playing a country-western tune, and on either side of the bar were several signs advertising brands of beer.

Joe walked over to the bar and ordered one of the

advertised beer brands. The bartender, whose nametag read "David Hu" set the glass in front of him. "Woman trouble?"

"How did you guess?" Joe gave the man a rueful smile.

"You had the look of a man who just tangled with a female."

"Tangled is about the size of it."

The bartender chuckled as he turned to another customer.

As Joe drank his beer, he studied the crowd around him. Lobstermen, a few tourists, and one teenager who watched him.

Joe turned back to the bar, ignoring the kid, while actually keeping an eye on him. He taught introductory biology, including lab, so he'd learned how to keep his attention on more than one thing at a time. On sharp objects or chemicals, for instance, as well as the students using those tools.

This boy was in his late teens or very early twenties. Dressed in jeans and a black T-shirt with a white zombie face on the front, he looked like the typical young person. His stance, though, and the way he looked around told Joe he thought he was badass.

He got those in his classes occasionally. Usually the parents were either clueless, or determined to get the kid on a straighter path. Either way, somebody insisted on college. Why, Joe could never figure out. He'd never seen one of those kids do well in class. Usually they were just a hazard in the lab, creating problems he had to monitor closely instead of helping the students who really wanted to learn.

Across the room, the kid gave him frequent, quick

glances out of the corner of his eye.

"Can I get you anything else?" Dave asked.

Joe leaned a little closer. "Any chance you know that kid over by the door?"

Dave wiped the bar for a moment, then his mouth tightened. "I don't know his name, but I've pitched that chowderhead out of here a couple of times. He thinks he's a big man, but for me he's underage trouble."

"Kinda what I thought."

"Well, hell, he's leaving. I won't have to throw him out."

Joe watched the kid out of the corner of his eye, and the last thing the boy did was shoot a final glance straight at him. Then he was gone.

"He seems to be overly interested in you," Dave said.

"I think I'll find out why."

Joe threw down a tip for the bartender and headed toward the door.

The boy turned the corner and Joe hurried after him, making sure to stay well back while not losing the kid. It turned out to be easy. The boy wasn't any better at not being seen than he was at watching somebody without being caught.

When the kid ducked into Justin's apartment building, Joe's jaw clenched. Not that he hadn't figured that's where the little jerk was going, but it angered him anyway.

He reached the third floor just as the boy was squatting in front of Justin's door, sticking some kind of flat piece of metal in the deadbolt keyhole.

"It'd be easier to use this." Joe held up the key.

For a second, the boy's eyes had a look that was

more like a man who'd seen too much than a young person. Then he shot to his feet. "You're dead!"

He stared at Joe for a moment before he spun and rushed for the exit.

Joe had no desire to chase anybody down two flights of stairs, so he turned to the door. There might be a few more scratches on the keyhole, but other than that, he saw no indications of any attempt to break in. He considered calling the cops, but decided against it. There was no proof the kid was anything but a snot-nosed wannabe looking for something to steal. In fact, that could be exactly what he was.

Except he didn't believe that for a minute.

Joe closed the door behind him, twisted the deadbolt, and dropped onto the couch. Was this boy part of a bigger conspiracy?

That sounded paranoid even in his head. That kid didn't seem like the kind of person a large organization would use. Was something else going on, something he wasn't seeing? Maybe something he was missing because he didn't have the whole picture.

Or because there wasn't anything to see.

Groaning, he let his head fall back to rest on the couch. He had no idea what his next step should be.

****

Kevin sat at one of the round computer tables in the town library. The Captain's Library, they called it. Odd, these Lobster Cove people. It didn't matter, though, as long as he had access to the computers—and the books. Not that he'd admit to any of the other guys that he checked books out of the library. They'd make fun of him.

He didn't care. Let them laugh. He'd heard

somewhere that knowledge was power. He believed that. If he discovered the right stuff, he'd have some power over the jerks that Vincent had doing whatever he told them to.

It only took a few minutes for Kevin to find several news articles about the murder of journalist Justin Sullivan. The story had been reported not only locally but in the national news too. Apparently this reporter dude, or journalist, or whatever he was, was a "rising star", whatever that meant.

It appeared the guy was really dead, but if he was, who was it running around town looking exactly like the reporter dude? Kevin was determined to make sense of things.

After much searching, the Internet gave up the secret. Justin Sullivan had a twin brother named Joe. It was right there in an article about some journalist awards dinner.

Kevin stared at the picture. With the reporter and his brother standing side by side, he could see some differences. After he'd studied the picture for a while, he saw enough differences to know it was the dude's twin brother he'd seen around town, who'd followed him to the reporter's apartment.

He printed the article with the picture, and headed out. He had something important to talk about to Vince.

****

"Her hair is gorgeous." Tim gushed.

Charlene sighed. "It really is."

"If you say so." Veronica eyed herself in her dresser mirror. Truth be told, she was rather proud of her long, silky, blonde hair.

"Oh, I say so." Behind her, Tim slid the hairbrush

through the strands, letting out a sigh every now and again. "I'd kill for this hair."

Charlene giggled.

"It'd go great with your best suit," Veronica said.

He groaned. "You just have to do that logical, scientist thing and ruin a perfectly good fantasy."

Veronica grinned at his woeful expression. "I'm sorry."

"No, you aren't."

"I wish my hair was beautiful like yours." Charlene leaned toward the mirror and pulled at a curl.

Before Veronica could say anything, Tim was behind the kitchen chair her sister sat in, and running his hands through her shoulder-length hair. "Girl, those curls are adorable! They're every bit as to-die-for as your sister's long hair."

"You're just saying that."

Tim put a fist on one hip. "Honey, I am the type of person who tells it like it is, especially when it comes to beauty."

"But I can't do anything with it. Besides, this stuff is boring brown."

"Oh my heavens. The two of you are in serious need of beauty guidance."

"Good thing you're here for us." Veronica managed not to grin.

"Well, you don't have to be sarcastic. And yes, it is fortunate that you have someone with my skill set to guide you."

He shoved his fingers into Charlene's hair again. "This is not brown, my fledgling. This is mocha and crème brûlée with a touch of cinnamon and a sprinkling of ginger."

"Are you serious?" Charlene's eyes were wide.

He put both fists on his hips and gave Charlene a narrow-eyed look in the mirror. "As for the curls, you can grow long hair, but curls are a nightmare to fake. Be proud of your hair."

"Really?"

Tim gave a slow shake of his head. "Honey, I told you already. When it comes to matters of the hair, face, and body, I am disturbingly frank."

Veronica put a hand over her mouth, but she couldn't completely stop the laugh.

Tim rolled his eyes.

Charlene brushed her curls in one direction, then another. "I don't know what to do with this stuff."

Tim took the brush from her. "The first thing is to set you up with a good stylist. You'll have to go into Bar Harbor, but Georgie frequently works odd hours, so sunlight won't be a problem. Then you and I will have to work on how to maintain."

"Thanks, Tim."

"Oh it's my destiny to cultivate beauty." He looked in the mirror at her, his eyes narrowing as he tapped the edge of the hairbrush against his chin. "You know, you two should come down to the club one night after the show is over. The girls would love to show you a few things."

Veronica stared at him. "I thought you divas were insular and protective of your territory."

"Honey, this is Lobster Cove. If we didn't get along we would have killed each other long ago." He leaned forward so his head was between the two women. "Please don't tell. If the truth got out, we'd be the laughing stock of the drag queen world."

"Your secret is safe with me—along with all the rest." Veronica squeezed his arm.

"Me too." Charlene said.

"I'm just happy I can be myself with the two of you."

Veronica smiled. "And we can be ourselves with you."

"As long as you don't bite me."

Laughing she rose from the chair. "You know we don't bite."

"Yeah, yeah, I know. You don't have fangs either." He shook his head sadly. "Figures, I know real vampires and they don't even have fangs."

"I know a real drag queen, and he doesn't even have catfights with the other queens. What a rip-off." Veronica grinned at him.

"Hey, I didn't say never. I just said we mostly get along."

"Ooh, well that's interesting."

Tim rolled his eyes. "Oh, go to work. I have things to do at home. I'm reading this great romance, *The Prince's Revenge* by Scarlette LaFlamme."

"I've heard of her," Charlene said. "She's a local."

"But nobody knows who she really is," Tim said.

"I know, she could be anybody. That's so cool."

"Isn't it?" Tim was all but vibrating.

"You two are weird," Veronica told them.

"We love you too," Tim said, then grinned and hugged her. "Actually, I do love you, you know."

Veronica kissed his cheek. "What would I do without you?"

"Your life would be *so* boring."

She sighed. "I'm glad you're my friend."

"Mine too," Charlene said.

He tugged one, then the other into a hug, then turned and headed out the door.

Veronica quickly pulled her hair back into a utilitarian ponytail. "This will just have to do for now."

Charlene hugged her. "This was fun."

"We need to do fun things more often."

"Yep." Charlene grabbed her bag and headed out the door.

Veronica gathered her things, but before she left, she took one more look in the mirror. Left side, right side, front on, big smile. She was still smiling when she walked down the sidewalk toward her job.

****

"I don't understand, Joe. Why is it taking so long for them to release Justin's body?"

Joe stood in the living room of his brother's apartment and tried to find the words to comfort his mother. Meanwhile his own heart tore into confetti. "Mom, they're doing everything they can to find the person responsible for what happened."

"What happened?" His mother's indignant voice came through the cell almost as strongly as it would be with her standing right beside him. "You mean the man who killed my baby and left him lying on a cold beach all alone? That's what happened?"

So much for trying to be sensitive. "Mom, they need to make sure they aren't missing anything."

"It's been four days. What could they be missing?"

Joe searched his mind for something reassuring to say. In the end he stuck with, "I don't know."

"I don't want to have to bury my boy, but if I have to I'd prefer to get it the hell over with." The breaking voice all but had Joe on his knees.

"I'll check again, Mom. That's all I can do."

"Thank you, Joe. I'll be glad when you get back. Family needs to be together right now."

"I'll be back as soon as I can."

"You do that."

They hung up, and Joe stared out the window toward the lights of Lobster Cove. He didn't want to go back until he had some answers, but he had to take his brother home and be at the funeral. He had to know his brother was safely put to rest.

He turned and forced himself to put down the cell before he threw it against a wall. Damn, their mother shouldn't have to go through this. No mother should.

He would take his brother home and take care of his mother. After that, he would find the answers, even if he had to question every person between here and China. He intended to make damn sure somebody paid for hurting Justin.

****

Veronica stared in shock at the disaster that had been the lab. Computers smashed, broken glass all over the floor, centrifuges, test tubes, boxes open and contents scattered, PCR and other specialized processing equipment trashed. Blue gloves scattered like decorations.

"Oh my God!" she whispered. "Why would anyone do this?"

"A better question," Dr. Wright said, "is how humans knew about the lab in the first damn place."

"A human has been hanging around the parking lot," Todd said. "I've seen him talking to Veronica."

She turned to give Todd a hard glare. He was

slimy, but she'd had no idea he'd stoop to this level. He crossed his arms over his chest and raised an eyebrow at her.

"Veronica, would you like to explain?" Dr. Wright asked.

Not really.

Taking a deep breath, she kicked up her chin and prepared to lie her butt off while keeping as close to the truth as she was able. "The human Todd saw is one who believes I know something about his brother's murder, but I don't."

"Something about *what*?" Dr. Wright gave her a hard glare.

"His brother was killed, and he thinks I know something about what the police are doing."

"Why would he think that?"

She swallowed, trying hard not to clench her fists. Focus on plausible, she told herself. She wasn't allowed to talk about her work for the Guardians. "Because he saw me at the shore where his brother was killed."

"What were you doing there?" Dr. Wright's glare hadn't wavered.

I was speaking with the coroner."

"Another human?" Todd's nostrils were flaring.

"We sometimes discuss her more interesting cases, scientist to scientist."

"That's absurd!"

Dr. Wright turned his glare on Todd. "Why don't you start cleaning up?"

Todd gave Veronica another hard look, but even he wouldn't risk Dr. Wright's rage.

Her boss turned back to Veronica. "So this human knows where you work"

"He's following me around like a puppy looking for crumbs. He's probably doing the same to everybody who was at the scene. His brother's death seems to have affected him strongly. So much so as to cause irrational behavior."

Sorry, Joe.

Dr. Wright looked anything but convinced. "You were at the scene of a human's death?"

"Yes, sir. It was an interesting case." She shrugged.

He leaned closer. "Do you think this human might be the one who broke in here?"

Her incredulous expression was genuine. "Of course not. He's a grieving human who isn't thinking straight. He couldn't have gotten through our defenses, and would have no reason to try."

The boss nodded. "I agree. I think we're dealing with one of our own."

"But there's the scent of human in here," Todd said.

Dr. Wright nodded. "I believe a human was involved, but only a vampire could do this without leaving a trace."

"Why would a vampire and a human cooperate?" An artery pulsed in Todd's neck.

"Perhaps the vampire used our ability to compel a human, thus preventing our knowing exactly what happened." Dr. Wright turned and walked over to where Todd pretended to clean. His expression wasn't a pleasant one.

Veronica pulled out her cell, which had vibrated twice during the conversation. A quick look told her it was Joe calling. She turned off the phone and went to work. Talking to him right now was not a good idea.

He'd just have to wait.

She would not admit to missing him.

Chapter 6

Joe sat with his arm around his mother and tried to listen as a minister, who hadn't laid eyes on Justin for at least a decade, said nice words over his casket. By the shaking of her shoulders, he knew his mom was silently sobbing, and he hoped the minister's words gave her some comfort. All he could think about was his brother's killer walking free.

The smell of fresh earth swirled around him, while friends and family stood or sat with their heads down, each in their own way mourning the loss of a man so young, so vibrant, so full of promise.

It was all so surreal, the formal ending of his brother's life. Joe's insides were empty, like his organs were in that casket with Justin. When the service was over, it took everything he had to leave his twin.

It tore him up inside, but he managed to lead his mother away from the site and toward friends and family. With a glance over his shoulder at the casket, he silently swore he'd somehow make sure Justin's murderer was brought to justice.

That was later, though. Right now, he needed to help his mother get through this long, hard, horrible day.

A hand clamped down on his shoulder, and Joe looked into the eyes of one of his two best friends.

"How're you doing?" Nate Warren asked.

"Hanging in there. I'm surprised you're in town."

"I told my boss this funeral was a priority." The look on his friend's face told Joe he wasn't joking.

"Thanks."

"Just let me know if you need anything."

Joe nodded as he wondered what his friend would say if he asked him to help track down a murderer. Before he could think too much more, an elderly aunt pulled Joe into an embrace.

An hour later, the crowd had moved to his mom's house. The house he and Justin had grown up in. Very little had actually changed over the years, and the things that had were mostly superficial. Different furniture in the living room. Updated appliances in the kitchen. But the same kitchen table where he and Justin had done their homework.

Food was everywhere, and Joe was shocked to realize he was hungry. Throwing a few things that looked halfway appetizing onto a plate, he found a corner to eat. It seemed wrong to satisfy a need that Justin no longer had. When a laugh came from the crowd, it was all he could do not to scream at the lack of respect. How could anybody be happy today?

"Is there anything I can do?" Nate put a hand on Joe's shoulder.

"No, but thanks. I appreciate you being here today."

Nate sighed. "I have to leave for Arizona in a couple of hours. You have my cell number. give me a call if you need anything."

Joe watched his friend weaving through the people filling the little house. "I need you to help me find Justin's killer," he muttered.

It was unfair, he knew. Nate had a high pressure job that required almost constant travel.

Determined to let the unreasonable resentment go, he forced himself to move around and greet their guests. His mom needed support from the family and friends who had come to mourn with them. The least he could do was thank them for coming.

The next few hours were an emotion-twisting blur, as he focused on being polite while wishing everybody would go away so he could nurse his grief in privacy.

"You doing okay, Joe?"

He turned to see a familiar face and managed a weak smile. "Good to see you, Michael."

"Sorry I wasn't at the funeral. I had an emergency surgery."

Joe noted the blue scrubs his friend was wearing. "I understand. How're Lyndsy and the girls?"

"They're fine." Dr. Michael Silver leaned closer and lowered his voice. "What did you find out about what happened to your brother?"

Joe sighed. He didn't want to go into the whole, ugly mess, but the idea of sharing the burden with a friend—and finding out what that intelligent, thoughtful friend thought of the oddness he'd stumbled on in Lobster Cove, did sound good. "Let's take a walk."

Michael nodded, and the two of them slid out the back door and headed down the side road they had walked together many times on their way to elementary school.

"So what's going on?"

Joe filled his friend in on the events of the last few days, leaving out the crazy attraction to Veronica. By the time they stood leaning against the fence around their old elementary school playground, he wondered if his good friend was thinking of throwing a net over him. Could surgeons certify a guy nuts?

"You aren't buying all this vampire nonsense, right?" Mike asked.

"No. Not exactly." He groaned. "I honestly don't know what to believe anymore. All I know is that Justin's dead, and he believed these vampires existed."

"This is beyond weird."

Joe hesitated, then dove in. "The woman I told you about, Veronica, she can hear my thoughts—and I can hear hers."

"She's using some kind of trick."

"No, there's no way it could be a trick. Trust me. it was a very strange experience."

"So you and a woman shared a psychic moment. Hard to swallow, but maybe not as crazy as the rest of that stuff."

"Mike, Veronica is a vampire."

His friend froze for a second, his expression blank. Then he shook his head. "You're being conned."

"No. I don't know what the truth is about these people, but I haven't seen any evidence of a con."

Mike stared toward the road, his eyes unfocused for a long few minutes. "Odd stuff, that's for sure."

"I don't think the police will find Justin's killer."

Mike's gaze shot to catch Joe's. "Why? Because of this conspiracy and vampire stuff? That probably has nothing to do with what happened to Justin. Much more likely it was a random event." His hand gripped Joe's shoulder. "I'm sorry, buddy, but driving yourself crazy like this isn't helping. Not you, and not your mom."

"I don't want to hurt Mom, but the guy who killed

my brother has to be brought to justice."

"Joe, you're a professor, not a cop."

"I know that."

"But you're going back anyway."

"I have to. I owe it to Justin."

"I don't know what you think you can accomplish that the cops can't. Are you sure this is what you want to do?"

"Yes. I've already made arrangements for somebody else to cover my classes for the next few weeks."

Surprise crossed his friend's face. "Next few weeks?"

"I don't know how long this thing will take."

Mike looked at the ground, poking at a stick with the toe of his sneaker. Joe figured his buddy was gearing up to lecture him on reality.

Then Mike met his gaze. "I'm going with you."

Joe wouldn't have been more surprised if his friend had told him he could fly. "You can't do that. You're a doctor with a family. You can't just take off, you have responsibilities."

"I'm not letting one of my best friends get himself involved in a crazy conspiracy vampire thing without anybody to watch his back."

"You have a wife and kids. I don't know what's going on, but it could be dangerous."

"Exactly why you need backup."

"Mike…"

"When are you leaving?"

"Tomorrow morning."

"Does your mom know?"

"Yeah. She's not happy about it, but she

understands."

"I'll be on that plane with you."

Joe nodded, and they walked back toward his mother's house. He was glad for the support, but he'd just buried his brother. Putting his friend in danger seemed wrong. If it had been Nate—single, with a crazy job that had him on the road constantly—it might not have been so bad. But Mike?

He was determined, though, and Joe needed help. If nothing else, Mike could offer a fresh perspective. Lord knew he needed one.

Could this thing get more complicated?

****

Veronica had a lot on her mind as she hurried along the southwest edge of the town on her way home. She registered the banners and posters announcing the Harvest of the Sea festival without really seeing any of it. The only human business she was interested in was Justin Sullivan's murder.

Not that most vampires would call his death murder. Humans were looked upon as animals by her people. Vampires considered themselves to be superior in every way to humans, to be the ruling class of the planet. Even her own colleagues, who had seen the same DNA studies she had, considered the tiny genetic difference enough to make them a totally different species. A more evolved species, of course.

Her thoughts were interrupted by the feel of another vampire behind her. She turned and the man stepped out of the shadows.

"I would like to speak with you," the red-headed, medium height vampire said.

"About what?"

"About the death of the human named Justin."

Curiosity flared, along with a good dose of distrust. "Why come to me?"

"Because you work with the Guardians."

She fought to maintain a neutral expression. "Why would you think that?"

He shot a glance around them and lowered his voice. "Because I saw you with a Guardian."

Anger flared inside her and tightened her jaw. "You've been watching me?"

"Actually, I saw you at the shore where Justin lay dead." He closed his eyes for a moment while an expression of anguish crossed his features. "Then I saw his brother talking to you. I was looking for Joe when the Guardian went into your building." He shrugged. "I only knew that he came to talk to you by your reaction just now."

She groaned. Stealthy she wasn't. "Okay, so what do you want from me?"

"I want your help finding Justin's killer."

She studied him for a moment, edged at his mental barriers but quickly discovered she wouldn't be able to breach them without force. "Why do you care what happened to this human?"

"I was his lover."

Surprise pulled at her. "You're admitting to a sexual relationship with a human?"

"Not just sexual. We were *Linked*."

Veronica's mouth dropped open and she snapped it shut. Forcing a neutral expression, she slammed the door on her errant thoughts. "That's impossible."

"That's what I always thought too. Until it happened to me." He took a small step toward

Veronica. "Look, believe me or not, I don't care which. All I'm interested in is making sure his murderer doesn't go unpunished."

"Murderer?"

Conner's expression went dark. "Why not use that word? If we are alike enough to be *Linked*, we are alike enough to have respect for each other. To use the same terminology for loss."

"So you really cared for this human?"

His chin shot up. "Yes, I did. And I want to see the vampire who killed him pay."

"You think I can help you with that?"

"I think you are in a position to discover facts that could lead to the identity of the killer."

The pain and anger slipped from beneath Conner's shields, and she realized what he was planning. "If you take revenge for a human, your life could be forfeit."

"Not just a human, Justin was my Beloved. I have the right to avenge my Beloved."

Veronica put a hand on Conner's shoulder. "A human—and a male. The Guardians will not recognize your right."

Anger blew hard from him as he shoved her hand away. "I don't give a damn what the Guardians think. The right to avenge a Beloved stretches back into the dark reaches of our history."

She watched the mix of anger and grief play out in the man's eyes. Her heart hurt for him, but reality was reality. "What you do or don't do is your business. I just don't see how I can help you find this killer."

He visibly pulled back the emotion until his shields were once again blocking her prod and his face was dispassionate. He looked into her eyes. "As I said, I believe you can find facts that are not generally available. Facts that the Guardians choose to keep to themselves."

A little piece of Veronica believed him, wanted to help him. "I don't know what you think my relationship with the Guardians is, but I don't have access to any secrets."

"I think you do, or could if you were motivated to look for them." With that, Conner turned and moved away with a speed a human would see as a blur.

She just couldn't get away from this human's murder.

"Damn," she muttered as she headed toward her apartment.

****

Joe's fingers shook as he dialed Veronica, but he ignored the reaction. He had to hear her voice. He was irritated because she hadn't answered her phone three days ago, when he had called to tell her he was taking Justin's body home. But he was worried too. What if the reason she hadn't answered was she was hurt or sick?

Or didn't want to talk to that crazy human who somehow could share thoughts with her. Maybe he should just hang up before she answered. Save himself the embarrassment.

"Joe, hi! How are you?"

Her voice sent thrills through his body straight to his lower regions. "I've been better. It's good to hear your voice."

"I'm so sorry I didn't answer when you called. We had a problem at the lab and I was tied up."

"It's okay."

"No, it isn't. I thought you'd call again, or we'd run into each other. It wasn't until yesterday that I found out your brother's body had been released for burial. I thought of calling you, but I'm unsure of human rituals and expectations. I didn't want to bother you. Are you okay?"

Why did he feel so glad that she'd thought about him? "I've been better, but the funeral is over now. Thank God."

"I…um…I suppose you'll be staying in Tennessee?"

He heard the sadness in her voice, and it had him smiling. Man he was screwed up. This was hardly the time to be strung out on a woman. "Actually, I'm coming back to Lobster Cove. I have to see this through."

"You mean find your brother's killer."

"Yeah."

A long sigh came from the phone. "Oh, Joe. Please let the authorities handle the investigation."

Irritation blew through him. "What investigation? Seems to me nothing is being done."

"They aren't going to tell you everything."

Something about her voice, or was it that he was still tapping into her thoughts? "You don't believe they'll find the guy any more than I do."

"I don't want you to get hurt." Her voice caught, and his heart twisted.

"I'll be fine. I'll see you soon."

"Be careful, Joe."

"I will." They hung up, and he wondered how he could be so taken with this odd woman.

And what it was she was not telling him.

****

Kevin lay sprawled in his bed reading the latest Stephen King novel. It had been days since he'd told Vincent what he'd learned about the dead reporter having a twin brother. He'd been sure Vincent would be glad to have the information, but little had been said, and Kevin all but itched with irritation. He'd found out something important, damn it!

Voices rumbled from the living room, and he focused on tuning it out. Then he heard somebody say something about a reporter, and he slid off the bed and edged into the hall where he could hear.

"So that nosy reporter has a brother, a twin, actually," Vincent said. "So we're gonna need to keep an eye on him."

"Do you think he'll be a problem?" Luke asked.

"Probably not, but his brother could have told him something to make him suspicious. He's a biology professor at some little college, not a reporter or anything."

"Good you found all that out, Vince," Luke said. "You're so smart about things like that."

"Knowing what's going on and dealing with it is just part of being a leader."

Kevin ground his teeth as he went back to his room, hid the book, pulled on his hoodie, and slipped out into the cold night air. He would never get any respect here. Not from Vincent or the other guys. Maybe he should go somewhere else, do something else.

Maybe the crazy lady was right.

****

By two the next afternoon, Joe had listened to the

Bar Harbor sheriff spend an hour explaining why he had no suspects in Justin's murder. The police force was doing everything in their power to find the culprit, the man kept saying. In truth, Joe believed they were trying. Several things about his brother's death didn't add up. Things the Bar Harbor police probably wouldn't take seriously. Hell, he wasn't sure how much of the emerging story he could accept.

After leaving the sheriff's office, they went to the morgue. Joe vaguely remembered the coroner from the night Justin died, but most of that awful experience was blurry in his mind. He'd remembered a woman, but hadn't remembered she was tall, slim, and looked nothing like any coroner he could have imagined.

Mike, on the other hand, wasn't stressed, so he noticed immediately how she looked. To give his married friend credit, if the conversation was any indication, he was much more interested in the woman's brain than her body.

Joe wasn't interested in either one, and after almost an hour of listening to Mike and the coroner trade medical words, he was ready to walk out. They might enjoy getting nowhere on a four-syllable trip, but he just didn't frigging care. Unable to handle the frustration, Joe got to his feet and went to stand at the single window in the coroner's office.

"Mr. Sullivan?" the coroner came toward him. "I understand that this must be hard for you."

Irritation bit at him like fire ants. "I understand that nobody has any damn idea of what happened to my brother. You and the sheriff want me to believe you'll find the bastard who killed him, but we both know you won't."

Mike stood. "You do realize it isn't Dr. Hutchins's job to find the bad guy. She just—"

"It's all right." The woman's voice wasn't loud, just commanding. Mike sat down.

The coroner put a hand on Joe's shoulder. "I know you're upset, you have every right to be. I wish I could tell you that I have the magic clue that will solve the case, but I don't. I do have materials still in the testing process. Maybe something will come of that."

Joe met her gaze. "But you don't think it will?"

She smiled. "I've done this job long enough that I know better than to guess. I promise you that if I do find something, I'll keep you in the loop."

"Thank you, Dr. Hutchens."

"Call me Pat, please."

Joe smiled in spite of himself. "Thank you, Pat."

"You take care." She turned. "It was nice meeting you, Dr. Silver."

"Please call me Mike. Nice meeting you too."

Pat and Mike shook hands before the two men headed out the door.

"She's a very knowledgeable woman," Mike said. "I was impressed."

"What did you expect?"

He shrugged. "I don't know. it's not like I meet a lot of coroners. But whatever I might have imagined, she wasn't it."

Wait until you meet Veronica.

"I guess we might as well get back to Lobster Cove. I think we've done everything we can here."

"Are you sure it wouldn't be better to just go home and let the authorities handle this?"

Joe's last nerve snapped and he spun to face his

friend. "Did you hear the same thing I did? Because I didn't hear a whole lot of anything except excuses."

"You have to know they aren't going to share everything with us."

"*Everything?* "They didn't share shit. Mostly because they don't know shit."

Passers-by turned to look at him, but Joe was too raw to care. "Justin's dead. Gone. Buried. His throat cut and his blood all over the ground. You really want to tell me that I should just go home like a good little boy and let the clueless authorities handle things?"

Mike got right in his face. "Do you really think you can do better? You're a biologist turned professor, what the hell do you know about solving a murder?"

"I have Justin's research. He was convinced something strange was going on and he did a damn good job of documenting his theory."

Mike blinked, then leaned closer to Joe. "You have papers that could help the police and you haven't handed them over? What is your issue?"

Joe pulled his friend to the side of a building where they'd be out of earshot. "Do you really think the cops would be interested in a conspiracy theory involving creatures that he calls vampires? What would they think of Justin? That he was crazy maybe? That he was killed by another crazy?"

"Have you ever considered that maybe he was?"

Joe clenched his fists. "Was what?

"That maybe, just maybe, your brother was a little unconventional?"

White hot anger blew through him, and he acted on it before he thought. His fist and Mike's face intersected. Hard.

The other man stumbled back and held up both hands in surrender. "Chill, buddy. I didn't mean it like that."

"Then how the hell did you mean it?"

"I just meant that Justin might have been a good target for a con. He was always a little, well, different."

Joe took a step toward Mike, who still held up his hands. "You'd better not be going where I think you are."

"No, not because he was gay. Because he always had an amazing imagination and wanted to believe in spaceships and aliens and stuff."

"That's when we were kids." He took a step toward Mike, and Mike backed off again. "You know what? I think you don't want to fight because you're afraid of hurting your delicate surgeon's hands."

"Well, honestly, that is a consideration."

Joe shook his head. "You always were a wuss."

Mike grinned. "A wuss who makes more in a week than you do in a year."

"Smartass."

"Better a smartass than a dumbass."

"Let's go back to Lobster Cove." Joe turned and headed down the sidewalk.

"Fine with me. I want one of those lobster rolls I keep hearing are so good."

"They are yummy." He grinned. "But you don't pronounce the r's. More like lobsta."

Laughing, they headed toward Joe's rental car. Still, deep in Joe's thoughts, a tiny doubt lay. Had Mike really come with him to help, or to make sure he hadn't followed his brother over the edge?

****

If she did this it could get her into trouble. Big trouble.

Veronica stared at the papers fanned out over her kitchen table—the report she had done for the Guardians. She always kept both an electronic and hard copy, just in case. The scientist in her insisted.

Her carefully composed report lay before her. She'd included her careful observations and listed every sample she'd taken, every test she'd performed. Including the DNA samples. One from the victim. One foreign—taken from the area of the small cut on the victim's neck. The one where a male vampire had put his mouth to drink blood. The DNA profile of Justin Sullivan's killer.

Of course, without another profile to compare it to, it was worthless.

With a huge sigh, she leaned back in the chair. It seemed everybody thought she could help, but what could she do? She had written her report as carefully and completely as she could and turned it over to the Guardians. It was their job to handle the situation. Only the Guardians had the power to impose any kind of punishment on a vampire—and they didn't see a problem with a human being killed. If she ignored their judgment and dug around for information, she ran the risk of getting in very big trouble.

She'd always believed some ideals were worth risking trouble for. This, she decided, was one of them. One deep breath for courage, and she was ready to put her convictions to the test.

In seconds, the papers were once again in a neat file folder, and she'd booted up her laptop. Her cursor hovered over the Internet icon, but she paused to open her picture files.

The first photo was of two little girls, both wearing bright dresses and smiling happily at each other. Veronica and Linda Westin, her best friend in elementary school. Veronica took a moment to study the picture of the two of them at Linda's seventh birthday party, the moment frozen at a time when they'd both been happy. When neither of them realized just how horrible life could be.

Three months after the picture was taken, Linda was diagnosed with a rare form of leukemia. In fact, T-6 was the only type of blood cancer vampires could develop. One of the very few ailments vampire and human shared.

Linda had one more birthday. Only Veronica and another friend had gone to the hospital to help celebrate.

The memory of her beloved friend lying pale and sick against the white pillows still haunted her. Three days after that party, Veronica's mother told her that Linda was gone.

Wiping at tears that still burned, Veronica closed the picture file and opened the browser. It only took a moment to access the Guardian's system. She logged in and went to the area she used to input her reports. As long as she stayed here there was little to no risk. She could always say she was double checking that she'd filed something.

After Linda died, Veronica stood at her friend's grave and swore that she would devote her life to finding why this one disease could cross species lines and take vampire lives. She'd never backed down from that promise, devoting hours beyond her schoolwork to reading everything she could find about T-6.

It didn't take long to discover the wealth of information from human research into all forms of leukemia. From that discovery, it was a short trip to the knowledge of how many humans suffered and died. Not just from T-6, but from all the other forms of leukemia, the forms from which vampires were immune.

Shaking the memories from her head, Veronica resolutely clicked closed the reporting area and began a slow, careful search of the Guardian information bank. She'd had no idea of the incredible size and complexity of the stored data. That made sense, though. The Guardians were scattered around the world. Having immediate access to information twenty-four hours a day would make their jobs easier.

Most of the file names meant nothing to her, and she spent a long hour exploring the edges of the site. Folders, main files, files within files; it was all organized in some way that made no sense to her. She was about to give up and get out before she was discovered, when she clicked open one last folder and saw something that had her leaning toward the screen. DNA. The actual file name was "DNA processes."

"What the hell?" she muttered as she clicked the name. Convinced she was about to be unceremoniously booted from the system, shock sent hard, painful prickles down her arms when the folder opened.

Subfolders lined up in front of her. None were named, only numbered. At first they just seemed long string of digits. Then she realized the numbers either began with 13 or 14, and the last three numbers were always different, even when the middle numbers stayed the same. "Well hell, there's only one way to find out if

I can access anything."

Maybe the words gave her courage, or maybe she just couldn't take the curiosity any longer, whatever the exact rationale, she picked a random file and clicked the number. It opened.

For a moment, she simply stared at the file in front of her. It was a familiar sight, a computer- generated DNA sequence. "What the hell?" she leaned toward the screen, as if closer inspection would tell her why this type of information was on the Guardian site. It made no sense. None at all.

A quick scan of the sequence told her it was the genotype of a male vampire.

Okay. Now what?

She closed the file and opened another. Also male vampire. Then another. Female vampire.

She checked the numbers on the three random files, and found what she suspected from the beginning. The file numbers that began with thirteen were male, the fourteen were female.

She pulled back out and looked again. There were dozens of DNA sequences in the database. What in the world could the Guardians want with all that genetic information? Where had they come from in the first place? Was it possible the killer's DNA was among the sequences in the files? That was highly unlikely Then again, it was the only idea she had.

She glanced at the paper file lying on her table. It would take forever to manually check each male sequence against the one of the killer, and her laptop didn't have the software to do that kind of search.

The computers at the lab did though, and thankfully only the monitors were damaged during the break-in. Those had been replaced and the computers were up and running.

Her breath caught in her throat. That was a crazy idea. Was she determined to land herself in custody? Using Guardian resources that she had no right to be in was a seriously bad idea. She knew of no reason the killer would be in these files—unless the Guardians kept records of problem vampires. Even if she did find the right profile, she still wouldn't have a name. But it was something. Something was better than nothing.

Sighing, she got to her feet and grabbed a flash drive. In minutes she had copied the file with all the profiles to the drive. As fast as she was able, she got back to the area of the site she was allowed to access, logged out, deleted her history, and turned off her computer.

She sat for a long time, staring at the little piece of metal and plastic in her hand. Finally she dropped the flash drive in her purse. "This is the right thing to do," she whispered. Then she went to take a long, hot bath.

Chapter 7

"I have to admit, I haven't hidden in the bushes waiting for a girl since high school."

Joe glared toward Mike. He could barely see him in the dark. The trees they were standing beside all but blotted out the soft glow of the moon and the sharper beam of a nearby streetlight.

"Will you just be quiet, please? Veronica asked that we wait here for her. It'll only be a few more minutes."

"She's the vampire. Shouldn't she be the one hanging in the shadows?"

"I don't need the shadows." Veronica said from beside Mike.

Joe jumped as much as Mike, but it only took a moment for a smile to pull at his mouth. Even in the low light, he could see his friend's wide eyes. "I guess she got you, buddy."

"Damn, girl," Mike said. "Don't you make any noise when you walk?"

Veronica ignored him as she went over to Joe. "Sorry about the stealth. I don't think it's a good idea to be seen together right now."

As soon as she got close to him, Joe's breath quickened and his body hardened. Through the hormone induced reaction, he realized he sensed a strong emotion seeping from her. Worry? He touched her arm. "What happened?"

"We had a break-in at the lab. I've been seen talking to you in the parking lot." She shrugged. "I just thought it was better if we met somewhere else."

"So the first instinct is to blame the human, huh?" Mike asked.

Veronica turned to face him. "There is no doubt a human was involved."

"How can you possibly know that?"

She didn't even blink. "Humans and vampires smell different."

Joe decided to diffuse the situation. "What do the police say?"

She glanced down before meeting his gaze. "We don't involve human police in vampire concerns."

"Too big a risk," Mike said.

"Yes. I don't know how much you know about vampires, but we prefer not to reveal our presence to humans."

"So we won't know what you do to us?"

The emotion in Mike's voice stunned Joe. What was with all that animosity?

"If you mean drink your blood, yes, we do try to keep that quiet. The biggest reason, however, is that we attempt to live quietly among you. We try not to differentiate ourselves in any way."

"That makes it all right then? The blood drinking part?"

She didn't flinch. "The need to take in blood is no more right or wrong than you consuming food."

"We don't eat fellow humans—or vampires."

The bickering wasn't getting anywhere, and it gave Joe a headache. "Justin's journal said you only need to take in a little blood. Is that true?"

Veronica nodded. "Between one to three ounces every few weeks. It's possible to get by with even smaller or less frequent amounts, but that can lead to weakening and illness."

"Can't have that, can we?"

Joe glared at his friend. "What is your issue tonight?"

Mike shrugged. "It's creepy thinking about creatures drinking our blood."

"We aren't creatures. We are very much like you."

"Except for that pesky blood drinking thing."

Joe caught the other man's arm and tightened his grip. "Michael, stop!"

Mike shook his head, almost as if he were coming out of a dream. "I guess all those movies I've seen affected me more than I thought."

"It's a common issue," Veronica said, then turned to Joe and took his hand in hers. "How are you? I know it must have been incredibly difficult for you to bury your brother."

He squeezed her hand. "It was hell, but I'm doing okay."

"I'm so sorry you had to go through that. I can't imagine losing my sister."

A swirl of sadness washed from her over him, and his throat filled with answering emotion. He nodded.

She gently kissed his cheek. "Later." And she was gone.

"So you've been lusting after a vampire."

"Stuff it." Joe turned headed back to Justin's apartment. He had some hard thinking to do.

****

Veronica waited a couple of hours until Todd and Dr. Wright were focused on doing inventory of all the problems created by the break-in. She was working on inventory herself, but the flash drive in her pocket kept calling to her. She would be taking a huge risk, but it was at least something. Doing was definitely better than hoping things would work out. So she glanced once more toward the men, then walked into her office and closed the door.

Her hands shook, and it took three tries before she seated the end of the drive securely into the slot on the computer. She opened the DNA profile of Justin Sullivan's killer, and watched it fill the monitor screen. It wasn't an entire profile, of course. Full genotypes were rarely done. What was in front of her was more than enough to identify a vampire—or human, for that matter, though this profile was definitely vampire. Either way, it was enough to get her in big trouble.

Ignoring her trepidation, she set the software to compare key sections of the killer's DNA with those she'd copied from the Guardian database. Her heart threatened to beat right out of her chest as she sat the program in motion.

As soon as the comparison began, she pulled up an innocuous page from one of her latest reports. Pretending to read it, she worked on looking innocent.

The laugh was unexpected as it bubbled out of her chest. Her hand went automatically to her mouth, but nobody was within earshot. It was silly, trying to look innocent. In fact, that would probably get her caught faster than anything.

Leaning back in the chair, she closed her eyes and slowly convinced her body to relax. This was the right thing to do, and if she truly believed it was the right thing, then she had to be ready to confront the consequences head on.

Of course, there was no reason not to do everything in her power to prevent those consequences.

Pushing herself to her feet, she deliberately turned her back on the computer and strode into the lab. She had work to do.

****

Kevin spent the night working the streets, and by morning was almost four-hundred dollars richer. As he sat on a bench at the edge of the downtown park finishing his burger and fries, he kept an eye on the happenings in town.

When he saw that reporter's brother walking down the street, anger blew through him so hard he shook. Maybe it wasn't reasonable to be pissed at the guy, but Kevin didn't much care at the moment. He was as good a target as anybody, and Kevin seriously needed somebody to pound on.

He watched as the reporter's twin and a friend walked across Main Street toward Ned's Lobster Shack. Great, now there were two of them. Not that he couldn't handle two guys if he decided to, but who wanted to go all Jackie Chan when you didn't have to? Besides, if he decided to show that brother dude what was what, he didn't want to have to worry about some other guy getting in the way and taking his focus off the prize.

Maybe the friend would climb back under his rock soon. If not, then he'd come up with some kind of trick to separate the two. Yeah, that was the way to handle the situation. Be smart and make things easier on himself.

Kevin turned from his resting place and headed toward his favorite part of the woods. It was just outside of town, where he could keep tabs on things and still be alone. He'd stir up some trouble tonight. Yeah, trouble with a capital T. That's what he was good at, right? Maybe score an even bigger payday from a loaded tourist or two.

For a moment, his mind went to a picture of the crazy woman with the long blonde hair. She was just some nut. That's all. Just a loony tune woman. So he was a little freaked out. So what? He'd heard crazy people were stronger than regular people. He was smart not fighting her. That's all. He could have if he'd wanted to.

Kevin grinned as he headed toward the woods outside of town.

****

Joe tossed and turned for hours, finally giving up on sleep about four a.m. Sprawled on the couch, Justin's now familiar files covering the coffee table in front of him, his thoughts kept circling in the same pattern over and over. Were these vampires real? Was it true they had to drink human blood? Was the conspiracy against them real? Was that conspiracy what got his brother killed? Did Veronica know more than she was saying?

Sometimes he thought she was holding back. Was she? What was Mike thinking? Why had he been so hard on Veronica when he asked her all those questions? Why hadn't he asked those questions himself?

"Up already?" Mike asked from the hall.

"Couldn't sleep, so I decided to put the time to

good use."

"Are those Justin's papers?" Joe nodded and Mike came over and picked up a couple of the newspaper articles. "Looks like he did his homework."

"Why were you so ornery with Veronica yesterday?" The question was out before Joe had time to think.

"Ornery?"

"What would you call it?"

"I'd call it being a devil's advocate." Sighing, Mike sat and shoved a hand through his already messed-up hair. "I don't believe any of this vampire, blood drinking, mind reading, voodoo shit. I wanted to see what she'd say or do when I asked some serious questions."

"And now?"

"I think *she* believes what she says. And that you believe her."

Joe considered that for a minute, then indicated the pile of papers. "How about you look through this stuff, and I'll put on coffee?"

"Sounds like a plan."

Joe took his spinning thoughts into the kitchen. Maybe having another point of view would help clarify things. He hoped so, because he sure wasn't sure what was what anymore.

****

An hour before time to go home, Veronica slipped back into her office and checked the computer. Fully prepared for the search to be a dead end, it took her a moment to realize there was, in fact, a match.

It was only a number, but a quick scan of the profiles confirmed the computer had indeed found a matching profile to the one of Justin Sullivan's killer. She made a note of the number, removed the drive, cleared her history, and turned off the computer. The note and flash drive went in her pocket, and she went back into the lab to finish her work for the day.

She had a lead, but she had no idea how she could use it.

****

Joe set a cup of coffee in front of Mike. "What do you think?"

Mike took a sip of the hot liquid before he answered. "I still don't buy this whole creatures-of-the-night routine, but Justin definitely documented some kind of hate group. A far-reaching one, apparently."

"It seems to me something important to them is somewhere around Bar Harbor or Lobster Cove. Or at least they think it is."

Mike nodded. "Among several other places."

"True, but a lot of what Justin found seems to allude to something important in this area."

"Maybe that cute vamp girlfriend of yours."

Something grabbed at Joe's gut. "That's not funny."

Mike stared at him, eyes narrowed and questioning. "You really have a thing for her, don't you?"

He wanted to deny it, wanted to tell his friend how that was impossible, he couldn't feel something for a woman who either wasn't human, or believed she wasn't. Somehow he did, though. Somehow Veronica had gotten to him. He was fighting hard to keep from being sucked in, but he was pretty sure it was a lost cause.

His cell phone chirping pulled him out of his

confused thoughts. The number on the screen had him smiling as his heart missed a couple of beats. When he heard her voice, his whole body went hot and hard.

"Joe, I have something I think you need to see. It's too close to sunrise for me to go to you. Could you come over here?"

"I'll be right there," he told her, and clicked off the phone.

"Vampire calling?"

"Stuff it, Mike. I'll be back in a while."

"Have fun."

"Bite me," Joe muttered, and heard Mike's laugh as he went out the door.

****

Veronica sat sipping tea and wondering if she was doing the right thing. She knew by telling anyone what she'd done, she increased the odds that she'd get in trouble for it. It seemed to her, though, that Joe deserved to know she had a lead on the killer. It seemed a long time had passed since she'd called him, and she went to the front window to look. There he was, coming up the street. Her heart did a little jig, and she smiled. Okay, maybe deep down she might have had an ulterior reason for calling Joe. Maybe her discovery gave her a reason to see him. That wasn't so terrible, was it?

She caught a glimpse of him as he turned onto her road. He was hurrying along, and a part of her wondered if he was anxious to see her. Maybe. Or maybe he just wanted to know what she'd found out.

Movement to her right caught her attention a teenage boy edged along the side of the road from tree to tree. Recognition hit her. It was the kid she'd fed from in an effort to frighten him into a law-abiding lifestyle. If the look on his face was any indication, her efforts had been in vain.

The boy moved closer to Joe, and she realized what was about to happen. She grabbed for the light blanket she kept on the couch and threw it over her as she ran for the door.

****

Joe was almost to Veronica's apartment building when he caught movement through the foliage to his left. With his mind on her, and figuring it was an animal of some sort, he barely glanced in that direction. Which meant he was caught off guard when the teenage troublemaker dove at him from a small rise above the road.

The kid was heavy for such a skinny pain-in-the-ass, and he used coming from higher ground to his advantage. For a moment, all Joe could do was lie on his back and fight to get his breath while the kid pummeled him with punches. Then, with a gasp, air again filled Joe's lungs, and he wasted no time throwing a punch at the boy's ribs. It wasn't a hard punch, but it distracted him for a second, long enough for Joe to grab the kid's shirt with his other hand and haul him over to the side.

It only took a heartbeat for Joe to use the advantage. Shoving one knee against the kid's ribs, he ducked punches as he threw some of his own. Without the advantage of surprise, it didn't take long for the kid to resort to holding his hands in front of his face.

Joe stopped hitting, but kept his fists up. "What the hell do you think you're doing?"

The boy raised his chin. "Letting you know you can't screw with the Alliance of True Humanity."

Joe's breath caught as if he'd been knocked down again. Before he could question the kid, he heard someone run toward them and looked up. The sight of Veronica rushing his way, wrapped in a blanket, shot fear through him. Dawn had broken, sending long rays of light through the trees. She'd said she couldn't tolerate the sun. He wasn't sure what would happen, but he really didn't want to find out. Shoving the kid aside, he pushed to his feet.

"It's that crazy woman!" The kid scrambled to his feet, then turned and ran toward the trees.

Glad the kid was no longer a problem, Joe grabbed Veronica and turned her toward her apartment building.

"Are you all right?" she asked.

"Fine. You need to get inside."

He limped double-time up the steps into her building. They climbed the inside stairs with a peculiar two-step resulting from her trying to help him, and him trying hard to get her away from the windows and to safety.

Finally they made it into her apartment, closed and locked the door, then stood for a moment staring at each other.

"You're bleeding," Veronica said, touching a finger to a cut under his eye.

"I'll be fine. You're burned."

"Just a little. Let's get you cleaned up."

Five minutes later, they were in Veronica's tiny bathroom, her butt up against the sink, his shoulders against the shower curtain. She cleaned his wounds, and he gently smeared cream on the reddened spots on her face and hands.

They were so close. He could smell the strawberry

scent of her hair, hear her gentle breath, feel the warmth of her body. He went hard, but his stomach twisted with guilt that he could be so turned on when he was putting cream on burned spots on her sweet face. "Why in the world did you come rushing out into the sunlight?"

"I was scared for you."

"So you decided risking a serious burn to help me?"

"That little creep jumped on you."

Her wide eyes and the quiver in her voice had him smiling. "Sweetheart, I'm perfectly capable of handling one scrawny teenager."

"But you're…" she ducked her head.

He didn't need telepathy to know what she was about to say. "I may be human, but I'm far from helpless."

"I know," she whispered.

She looked into his face, and her warm green eyes seemed to touch him somewhere inside, where no one else had ever been. The temperature in the little room began to climb, along with his heartbeat. His gaze dropped to her mouth. She licked her lips and he almost lost it right there.

"Veronica," he whispered, and took her mouth with his.

Her lips opened to him, inviting him in, welcoming him to the soft warmth, letting him taste the sweetness that was uniquely her. He groaned as he tugged her body close. She fit against him like she'd been made for him. His hands slid down her back and cupped her rear. Perfect. He used his grip to pull her against him.

Her hands were active too, moving under his T-shirt and up the front of his chest. "Joe," she gasped against his lips.

"If we don't stop soon, I may not be able to," he managed to say."

"Who said anything about stopping?'

With that, he scooped her up and carried her out of the bathroom and across the hall into the only other room in the small apartment. There he laid her gently on the bed. "Sweet, beautiful Veronica," he whispered.

She smiled up at him, and he grabbed the hem of her top and tugged it over her head. Her bra closure caused his lust-addled mind a bit of thought, but it was soon following the top toward the floor. His shirt went over his head, with her help, and he grabbed her pants and slid them down her long, beautiful legs. She unzipped his jeans as he smiled in happy anticipation of the things he and this beautiful woman were about to do. Her breasts were the perfect size to fit into his hands, her shoulders were beautiful, her hips widened below her belly into a perfect woman-shape. Only the small, lace panties she wore stood between him and where he wanted to be with every atom in his body.

Her hand grasped his erection, and he gasped. "I think you need to come down here," she said.

He shoved his jeans and briefs to the floor, kicked off his shoes and slid into bed beside her. As their lips met, he slipped his fingers under the lace and touched her.

Her back arched and she moaned his name. "I want you." her voice was ragged.

Smiling, he lowered his head to her breasts and took first one, then the other nipple in his mouth. She hung onto his shoulders with both hands.

"More," she gasped.

He ripped her panties off and he stared at her with a desire so strong it was all he could do to hold off even a moment. Somehow he managed to pull away long enough to think. "Condom," he gasped.

"No need," she gasped back. "Different species."

He was too caught up in lust to think straight, but thought she must know what she was talking about. Good thing, because he wanted this woman so much it hurt.

She spread her legs and he slid into her. Long legs wrapped around his waist while soft lips worked some kind of magic on his mouth. They moved together until they reached a climax that should have set the room on fire.

He collapsed beside her. "Whoa."

She gently touched his face. "That was amazing."

He edged her close and kissed her forehead, her cheeks, her chin, her mouth. It only took a moment for his body to react to the touch of her sweet, soft body. "Veronica."

"I can't get enough of you," she whispered.

"We'll take it slow this time."

And he set out to kiss every inch of her.

****

"What the hell did you get yourself into?"

Kevin groaned. He'd hoped she wouldn't be home. "I had something that needed doing."

Shelly marched over to him and grabbed his shoulders. Damn, he hated it when she acted like she thought she was his freaking mother. "Who did you get into a fight with?"

He shrugged her hands off him. "I showed that brother dude who was boss."

"What 'brother dude'? What are you talking about?"

Frustration soared through him. "The brother of that guy who got killed. His twin."

The slap caught him off guard and he stumbled back. "What was that for?"

"For being an idiot. You should know better than to screw around in things that don't concern you."

"But I thought he might know something useful."

"Leave the thinking to the grownups, Kevin. You just do what you're told."

As he watched Shelly walk back to her seat in front of the TV, rage gripped him so hard he trembled with its power. Where did she get off acting so high and mighty? She was only a few years older, but she treated him like he was a baby. He could show her who was boss. He didn't have to put up with her. He was a man!

She turned and glared over her shoulder. "Don't get any ideas, kid. You know what Vince would do to you."

Kevin turned and went to his room. She was right. As long as he was with the group, he had to give in to the leader's demands, and he demanded that bitch of his be treated like she was more than she was.

It had seemed so cool, being in a movement that was working to protect the whole human race. More and more, being here seemed like being back in the damn foster homes.

****

The chirping of his cell phone pulled Joe from a warm, relaxing sleep. Reluctantly, he moved away from Veronica's warm body and reached over the edge of the bed to pull his phone from his jeans. "What?"

Mike's chuckle greeted him. "Sorry to bother you. When you didn't come back or call, I was a little concerned. But I guess you have things well in hand."

"Thanks for your concern. Later." As he clicked off the phone, he heard Mike's laugh.

"Everything okay?"

"Fine." He turned to Veronica and his body went hard again. "Better than fine."

"We're not going to be able to walk." She ran her hands up his chest.

His better sense managed to override his hormones and he sighed. "What exactly did you mean when you said we're different species?"

She shrugged. "Just that. We are different from each other."

He kissed his way down to one of her breasts and took the nipple in his mouth. "I don't know," he whispered against her. "You respond like a woman."

"Joe!" She gasped. "Can we talk about this later?"

Chuckling, he proceeded with his plan to see how many ways he could test her womanhood.

****

Kevin was coming back from getting himself a glass of milk when he heard Vince's voice. "What did the kid do this time?"

Shelly answered him. "He attacked the brother of that guy that got killed down in Bar Harbor."

"The guy who was trying to get dirt on us?"

"Yep."

Kevin peered around the doorframe into the living room.

"Did the kid say why he did a stupid-ass thing like that?" Vince turned and glared at Shelly. An artery in his neck pulsed so much Kevin could see it clear across the room.

"Said the dude might know something." Shelly licked her lips and her hands trembled.

Vince rubbed his forehead like it was killing him. "Well, if he didn't know something before, he'll be looking for something now. Damn, somebody solves our problem for us, and that boy has to go and stir shit up."

The boy, that's how Vince saw him, how they all saw him, and it wasn't right. He might be younger than the other members, but he was just as smart—smarter than most of them—and just as tough. Hell, he'd like to see Luke or Arnie live on the street. He'd bet his new jeans they wouldn't make it a day.

"Is there anything I can do, Vince?" Shelley asked.

Suck-up.

"Thank you, sweetheart," Vince was saying. "Right now, the only thing any of us can do is keep on track with the mission."

His gaze went to the window, as if he were looking out over a battlefield. "We have to stop those inhuman bastards before they destroy civilization as we know it."

Kevin turned and headed back to his room. Vince had promised him he would be part of something big, something important, something that would make a difference. So far, things were pretty much the same as ever. Except he was under Vincent's thumb instead of a foster parent's.

He didn't like being under anybody's thumb.

****

For the first time in her life, Veronica had a hard time focusing on her job. It wasn't just because she'd spent the day in bed with Joe, something else nagged at her. A thought was tingling in her mind, just below the surface, something she couldn't quite access. Something important.

A timer went off, and she forced her attention back to the next phase of extracting a DNA sample to process. As soon as the critical stage was over, she found her mind wandering back to that question she couldn't answer. When she shook that way, though, an even more unanswerable question floated into her head. What, she wondered, was pulling her so hard toward a member of a completely different species? It made no logical sense for her to be attracted to this human. No matter how similar the two species were, they were still different species. So why was she sexually attracted to this human? She should be attracted to vampire males, but none of them interested her. Not like Joe. But then, hormones didn't have logic, they just were.

It was almost an hour later before she realized what her heart had admitted when her logical brain refused. She wasn't just sexually attracted to Joe. She was somehow emotionally attached to him too. Logic argued that she barely knew this member of a different species. Her heart argued none of that mattered.

She sighed and leaned against the nearest counter. She had always prided herself on being a logical person, using her intellect to solve problems instead of making emotional choices, since those only seemed to get others, both vampire and human, into trouble. What had gone wrong this time?

Whatever the issue was, she had to get herself together. Now was definitely not the time to allow her emotions to cloud her judgment. Not when her career, and maybe lives, depended on her ability to think and act clearly.

****

Groaning, Joe dropped the journal on top of the pile of papers. "There's something I'm not seeing."

Mike handed him a cup of coffee. "Or something Justin didn't put in his journal."

"It's possible, I guess. I know that he left here in a hurry, he didn't empty his coffee grounds and clean the coffeemaker."

Mike's eyes widened. "Jeez, he *was* in a hurry."

"But I have no idea where he was going, or who he was meeting. I don't know if he went to the beach to meet his contact, or if he was talked into, or forced, to go later."

"Either way, the contact he went to meet could be his killer."

Joe nodded. "That's entirely possible."

"All that paperwork and nothing to indicate who he was meeting?"

"Not that I can see. You looked through this stuff, did you find anything?"

"No, but I thought maybe you did. I know that siblings, especially twins, sometimes see things nobody else does."

Joe looked at Mike. "How do you think I found this stuff?"

Mike sat beside him. "I still think you should turn all this paperwork stuff over to the police?"

"Which part do you think the cops would get a bigger laugh over, the mysterious conspiracy? Or the part about the inhuman creatures?" Joe looked at his friend's expression, and sighed. "That's what I thought."

"Joe, what if there isn't a conspiracy. What if this whole thing was a con out to separate Justin from his money, or to convince him to give somebody their fifteen minutes of fame?" He looked down as he said, "Maybe they killed him because he wouldn't cooperate."

Heaviness settled in Joe's gut. He leaned back against the couch and ran a hand through his hair. "I can't believe that. Justin was an experienced journalist. He wouldn't have been easy to trick."

Mike shrugged. "Under the right circumstances, any of us can be conned."

"Man, I wish the cops hadn't taken his phone and computer."

"Yeah, that does suck." Mike took a sip of coffee, then shook his head. "You know, Justin was so anal, he probably kept a record of all his meetings, but that info would have been on his laptop or maybe his phone."

Something clicked, and Joe slapped a hand to his forehead. "Justin never trusted electronic devices. He said it was way too easy for somebody else to get ahold of stuff."

"Like he did with these emails."

Joe looked at the printouts on the table as he nodded. "Exactly. So he wouldn't have left his most important information where somebody could get at it. He would have kept a paper record somewhere."

"Maybe in an address book, and the cops took that too."

"No." Joe closed his eyes for a moment, picturing his always-wary brother. Where would he keep the names of his contacts? In the safest place he could, of course. But where was that?

Then something he'd seen came back to him, and he rushed into the kitchen. "Peas."

Mike followed closely behind him. "What about peas?"

"Justin hates them." Joe pulled a bag of frozen green peas out of the freezer, as his stomach twisted. "Hated. He *hated* peas. Past tense."

"I'm sorry." Mike gripped his shoulder for a moment.

Joe closed his eyes and leaned against the counter until the pain lessened. Then he forced his attention back to the bag in front of him. Justin would sometimes split the seam on one side of some frozen food, then slide in whatever he wanted to hide. A little water along the seam and it was invisible.

Because the freezer door had been left open when the apartment was searched, it wasn't until the peas had partially melted that he found the sealed plastic bag that contained a piece of folded paper.

"Brilliant," Mike whispered.

"My brother was no slouch." Joe unfolded the sheet, and found names and phone numbers listed neatly down the page. Beside each name were dates and letters that had Joe smiling. Memories of cool autumn afternoons spent laughing with friends on their big back deck settled comfortably in his mind.

"What are the squiggles?" Mike asked, pointing at the writing beside the dates.

"Hebrew letters."

"Justin knew Hebrew?"

"A little." Joe's mind went down memory lane again. It was nice remembering good times with his brother. "Do you remember Aaron Jacobson?"

"Of course I do. He was the funniest kid in school. He lived next to you for a while, didn't he?"

"Yes, he did. Just so happened it was the year he turned thirteen."

Comprehension crossed Mike's face. "He taught Justin Hebrew."

"Actually he taught both of us. He was studying for his bar mitzvah, and figured out pretty quick that he learned faster if he taught us. We ate it up. It was different than our school lessons and that made it interesting."

"Sounds like fun. How come I never knew about any of this?"

"That was the year you and Nate played football, remember?"

Mike gave an exaggerated shudder. "I wish I could forget. Not my proudest hour."

Joe laughed. "Not so much."

"So while I made a fool of myself, you and Justin were having a great time?"

"Sorry." Joe grinned. "Aaron hated the work he had to do for Hebrew school, meanwhile, Justin and I wished we could have bar mitzvahs."

Mike snorted. "I can see it now, the Sullivan twins with yarmulkes on their heads and prayer shawls around their shoulders. Wow, those Irish Catholic grandparents of yours would have been so proud."

"Ha-ha, you're funny."

"I try."

By this time, Joe had fumbled through the dusty, cobweb-covered corners of his mind and remembered a couple of things. He pointed to one letter beside a name. "That's a *shin*."

"A what?"

"A letter. It sounds like either 'sh' or 's'."

"Maybe s for source?"

Joe nodded. "That's what I'm thinking. Most have that letter, so it makes sense."

"This one has two letters." Mike pointed. "What's that?"

Joe looked at the second letter. "A *mem*. For 'M'."

"Look at the date beside it, Joe."

He did, and his breath sucked in like he'd been sucker punched. "That's the day Justin was killed."

"M for meet?"

"That's a logical conclusion."

"So now we give this guy's name to the cops?"

Joe gave the idea serious consideration. He went over the pros and cons in his head. But there was only one way this could go. "If we had this much trouble figuring out where the information was and what he meant by it, people who don't know Justin are not going to take us seriously. We find this Kennedy guy ourselves."

"Damn." Mike sighed. "I was afraid you would say that."

****

The basement was always cold and dark. It was a little better now, though, because the heat of the men sitting in the four rows of chairs raised the temperature. The lights were all on too, including some installed just for the occasion. One light in particular aimed right at the front where Vince spoke. Kevin stood off to one side in the back of the room and listened.

"These *things* are not human, they are our enemy.

If we don't stop them, they will destroy us and our way of life. They take our blood. They take our humanity. They are animals who consider us prey."

A picture flashed through Kevin's head. A woman with long, blonde hair. The woman with that blanket thing over her head. The crazy one who ran to help the brother guy. She had to be crazy to come running toward a fight between men. But she was freaky in more ways than that. That same blonde who'd tried to help that brother dude had tried to help him. Yeah, maybe it was silly telling him to stop stealing and go back to school. As if. She'd tried, though, which was more than most people did for him. But she'd sucked his blood. How weird was that?

"We cannot allow the human race to be lowered to the level of cattle for the benefit of hell-spawned creatures!" Vince slammed his hand down on the table in front of him.

Kevin ran for the bathroom and barely made it before he lost his dinner.

Chapter 8

Veronica reached for her tea, only to find it had long since gone cold. Sighing, she got to her feet and took the cup to the microwave. While her tea reheated, she wondered if what she was doing wasn't a quick trip off the frying pan straight into the fire. Accessing the Guardian's data once was dangerous; to go back in and spend hours poking around was plain stupid. Was the remote possibility of finding a lead worth her career or even her freedom? Images of a dark, remote, scary Guardian prison teased her mind.

So why was she doing it? Why was something inside her so determined to poke into the hundreds of nooks and crannies of the database in an effort to find an elusive clue that might, or might not, help her make sense of the DNA profiles she'd found? Why put herself at risk when the odds of finding anything were miniscule? Even if she found out the name that went with the profile the chances of that making a difference were about one in a billion.

The microwave dinged, and she took her re-warmed tea back to the table. The truth was, she knew why, and it had a lot to do with her attraction to a human.

Rubbing her aching neck, she mentally argued with herself. She didn't like the idea that humans didn't matter. She wanted to see justice done, and only vampires could make that happen. If the killer was punished, it would have to be because somebody did something unsanctioned. And she seemed to be the only candidate.

Cons and pros, black and white, bad and good. She tried to make the decision logically. Tried to consider the consequences.

In the end, it was her heart that sent her back to the search.

****

Joe woke to loud snoring. He tried to sit up, only to have his neck protest moving from the cramped position he'd somehow fallen asleep in. Groaning, he forced his body to untangle from the corner of the couch and poked at the source of the snoring. "Wake up, sleeping beauty."

Mike snorted and pulled himself into a sitting position. "Damn, you snore like a bullhorn."

Joe eyed his friend. "And you don't?"

"Hell no." Mike yawned. "Damn, it's daylight. I'll make the coffee."

Joe laughed as he watched his buddy go toward the kitchen. Morning. Time to once again try to locate one T. Kennedy.

****

Veronica was on the verge of giving up and going to bed. The Guardian database was massive; with files labeled with random numbers and odd letters she thought came from a very old alphabet of the all but lost vampire language. These letters and numbers led to files within files. She might never find what she was looking for. Especially since she didn't even know what that was.

Clicking a link to yet another numbered folder, she found at least a hundred files linked inside. "Well, they don't have to worry about hackers. If somebody got inside here, they'd never find anything useful."

Hackers like her, for instance?

"I have permission to access this site." She shrugged. "Just not this section."

Her cell phone vibrating on the table startled her enough she almost fell off the chair. For a moment, she was sure she was caught. Then she looked at the display and let out a relieved breath. "Hello, Charlene. What's up?"

"Hey, Veronica. Mom's driving me nuts. Would you mind if I came over for a bit?"

The sound of her sister's voice seemed to lessen the tension in her head. "Sure, come on over. If you're willing to brave sunlight, it must be really bad."

They said their goodbyes, and she looked at her computer screen. She really didn't have time to do anymore now. Maybe after Charlene left she'd be more inclined to return to her headache-inducing search. She moved the mouse up to logout, but somehow wound up clicking on one of the links instead. A profile popped up. Picture, name, height, weight, all kinds of basic information—and of course more numbers.

Okay, now what? She closed that file and clicked open another. Another profile, but no indication as to why these files were where they were, or why they were labeled the way they were. She clicked again. This time the face in the picture looked familiar. Leaning closer to the computer she realized she knew the man. Sort of. He was a Guardian she'd met not long after she'd agreed to work with them. At least some of these were profiles of Guardians, but knowing that didn't help her much. Were all these files the profiles of Guardians, or was this guy in their database for some other reason?

The knock on her door called an end to her session. She logged out of the system, closed her laptop, and went to visit with her sister.

The mystery would just have to wait a little longer.

****

Joe dialed the number on Justin's secret list again, anticipating yet another direct link to voicemail. They'd spent half the day trying to speak to this Kennedy dude.

"The guy probably left the country," Mike said.

"Hello."

Joe almost dropped the phone when he realized he had an actual answer. "Hello, I'm calling for Mr. Kennedy."

"This is he."

"My name is Joe Sullivan. I believe you may have met my brother Justin."

A click signaled the abrupt end of the connection. Joe dropped his cell phone on the coffee table. "The bastard just hung up on me."

"Now what?" Mike asked.

"Damn if I know."

****

Kevin sat on a hill just outside the town and looked down at Lobster Cove. The place was almost like a scene out of a movie. Quiet. People mostly nice. And there was always that sound of the ocean. He wouldn't admit to it, but that sound comforted him.

All in all, Lobster Cove seemed like a nice place to live. If you had a real family, that is. That was something he'd never known. Sure he'd lived with his real dad for a while, but the man never cared whether there was food in the house, or the electric bill was paid, or if Kevin went to school in shoes that were too small and had more holes than leather. Nope, all his dad had cared about was the next bet, the next big payoff. Not that there ever was a payoff. Even if he won, his dad always put the money on another bet since he was "on a roll." If he didn't drink the winnings.

He took a bite of the burger he'd bought with the cash he'd stolen from that woman with the two screaming kids. It had been so easy. Those kids had her so distracted all he had to do was reach in the purse she'd left in her grocery cart and pull out the twenty he could see from a mile away. Dumb bitch.

That thought led to thoughts of another woman: The crazy blonde he'd tried to rip off. She had to be one of those creatures Vince called dangerous.

He had to admit, it was way beyond creepy, the way she'd sucked his blood. She didn't seem like a creature, though. Just a seriously weird woman. She seemed to honestly want to help him. Not that he was gonna do what she'd said, but just the fact she'd tried made her seem less like a creature. To be honest, in some ways she seemed more human than a lot of the humans he knew.

Except for that drinking blood thing.

He picked up his burger to take another bite, then hesitated. That blood thing still tangled his stomach up. He waited a minute for the feeling to pass, then went back to his good old, plain American food. None of that lobster crap for him, no sir. He wasn't about to eat something that looked like a big bug. In fact, he was about tired of this place altogether. Big bugs, icy ocean, cold air on the last day of September. Not just chilly, freaking cold. What kind of messed up was that? He wanted to go home to the South. Tennessee, Georgia, Florida even. That was more his speed. In fact, the warm ocean on the Florida coast would be the place to be this coming winter. Not here where it would be like the North Pole any day now.

He shoved the rest of the burger in his mouth and tossed the bag behind him before he headed down the well-worn trail through the woods toward the town. A lot of people were out about this time of day, coming in from sightseeing for lunch. Maybe he could pick a pocket or two. Or just enjoy feeling like he was part of the town, even if he never would be accepted anywhere as normal as this place. Fitting in had been a big attraction of the Alliance. Vince had made it sound so good, being a member of a group that was doing something important.

Damn Vince to hell. He was always saying people needed to take the initiative. Well, he had, and still he got treated like he was an idiot kid. This Alliance of True Humanity stuff wasn't all it was cracked up to be.

Why was Vince so mad because he'd beat up on that damn twin brother dude? What if the guy did have information about the Alliance? Didn't it make sense to show him what he was dealing with?

In fact, what difference did it make that he knew about them? If these bloodsucking people were really so dangerous, why wasn't the Alliance warning the public? Vince had been so worried about a reporter snooping around, but wouldn't that have been the perfect opportunity to get the word out? When he'd searched for information about the reporter dude, Kevin had realized the man was not just some nothing guy looking for a story to make his career. This Justin Sullivan already had a career. He was a successful journalist who had the credibility to get people to accept a crazy story about blood-sucking inhuman things. Now he was dead and the opportunity was lost.

Now Vince had his panties in a wad about this other Sullivan brother. Kevin's research said that Joe Sullivan was a college professor. A biology professor. Wasn't this another opportunity to be believed? What was Vince so worried about?

He was contemplating those questions when he glanced toward Main Street. The reporter's brother and his buddy walked along like they were big shots or something. Figuring he should take advantage of the opportunity, he strolled toward the men. Maybe he could get some good intel. Whether he shared the intel with Vince was still up in the air.

He was just about to catch up with the targets when he saw Vince coming from the other direction. Crap, he was about to get in trouble again. Great. Just freaking great.

He pulled his ball cap down and lowered his head. Maybe Vince wouldn't see him. He was about to head in the other direction when he realized Vince had stopped. Edging closer, Kevin tried to see without being seen. When he realized what was happening, he stopped worrying so much and moved close enough to hear.

"Dr. Silver, fancy seeing you in Maine." Vince was shaking the brother's friend's hand.

"Vincent Bolton, how are you?"

"I'm good," Vince said. "Isn't this place amazing?"

Dr. Silver looked around. "It's nice. Are you living here now?"

"For the time being. Haven't decided whether to stay long term or not. Depends on how business goes. You still saving lives back in Tennessee?"

"I'm still working as a surgeon," Silver said.

This was very interesting, but Kevin decided he'd better go before he was spotted. As he headed back to his favorite hiding place on the hill, where he could watch without being seen, he wondered at this new development. So the leader of the Alliance of True Humanity knew a friend of the brother of the dead reporter. What was it they said on TV? Oh yeah, the plot thickens.

****

"It was great spending time with you," Charlene said.

Veronica gave her little sister a hug. "I *am* the only person who understands about Mom."

"I can't believe she moved up here. I thought it was such a great idea telling her I was following you up here because I thought if there were opportunities for you, there would be for me." Charlene cringed. "When she said that was a great idea, and that she'd come too, I thought I would die."

"You like Lobster Cove, don't you?"

"Yes, I do. I love meeting new people from all over the world. I know Mom thinks I took the job at Sea Crest Inn just until I find something better, but I love working at that place."

"I'm glad you found something you enjoy."

"I saw a ghost."

"You saw what?"

Charlene laughed. "A ghost. I've seen her more than once, actually. She's a beautiful young woman who stands on the beach just below the Inn. She stares toward the sea like she's watching for a ship to arrive."

"That sounds sad."

"Maybe. I think it might be a sailor's wife waiting for her husband to come home. I guess he never did, or she wouldn't be haunting the beach. If that's true then yeah, it is sad."

Veronica shoved an unruly curl off her sister's face. "How do you deal with the no-sun problem?"

"Just told them I was allergic." She shrugged. "I put some of Mom's special facial stuff, that I really am allergic to, on my arm one day, then when I was nice and broken out, I told them I'd accidently exposed my arm to the sun. Took care of any lingering questions."

"I hate that lotion." Veronica scrunched up her nose as she remembered the scent. She keeps telling me it would do wonders for me. Yuck."

"Tell her you're allergic too." Charlene touched her arm. "I'm sorry she stays on you all the time about being girly."

"Doesn't bother me." Veronica touched her sister's hand. "But I know it bothers you when she nags you about losing weight, you're fine just the way you are."

"But not thin and long-legged like you."

She shrugged. "I don't understand the problem. My appearance is simply a result of the genes I inherited. Honestly, why we would want to adopt the human's skewed idea of what a woman should look like is beyond me."

"That's why I love you, Veronica. You always have something smart and logical to say."

"You love me because I'm your sister."

"That too." Charlene took her jacket from the hook by the door. "I'm heading out so you can get some rest. I know you have to work tonight."

"Be careful in the sun."

"Always." Charlene touched Veronica's cheek where a burn still healed. "Besides, I think you're the one who needs to be careful." She pulled on a jacket and a huge hat before heading out the door.

Alone again, Veronica was left to think about what she'd discovered in the Guardian's database. She told herself she needed rest, instead she found herself at her laptop logging back into the Guardian's info. She was close to some important new information. She just knew it.

"Oh good grief. Feelings aren't logical."

Logical or not, she spent the next several hours plodding through Guardian personnel files determined to see the logic to their system. And to use that insight to find if any of the files related to the DNA profiles she'd discovered earlier.

Even if it took her all day.

****

The sun was warm, even if the breeze coming from the ocean was chilly. Joe was comfortable sitting at the rustic wooden table outside while he and Mike ate their lobster rolls. The relaxing roar of the waves crashing, the sound of seagulls crying overhead, even the ubiquitous fishy smell he'd finally gotten used to, all of it was feeling familiar and good. He shook his head to clear that thought and focused on the present.

"So how do you know this Vince guy?" Friend of Mike's or not, something about the man rubbed Joe the wrong way.

Mike took a sip of his Coke before he answered. "His daughter was in an accident a few years ago. Hurt pretty bad. I was the surgeon on call, and I managed to save her life."

"So he thinks you're awesome now."

"I am awesome, thank you."

Joe laughed. "Yeah, and modest too."

"Enjoying your lunch, gentlemen?"

"Delicious," Joe told the middle-aged man standing beside their table. "Your food is always great." Across from him, Mike nodded agreement while chewing a huge bite.

Ned Rutherford owner of Ned's Lobster Shack, smiled. "Good to hear."

"Ned, do you happen to know a man named Kennedy?" Joe asked.

Ned frowned. "Sounds vaguely familiar, but I can't put a face to the name."

"Any idea who might know? It's kind of important."

The man thought for a minute. "You know, Charlie Burns might be able to help you. He's a lobsterman from way back. Finally got to the point where he couldn't work anymore, so he handed his business over to his kids and grandkids. Now he sits down by the pier and keeps track of everything going on. He probably knows everybody around here."

"Thanks, we'll talk to him."

Ned nodded and headed on to the next table.

Joe looked at Mike. "I think we should take a walk after lunch."

Mike sighed. "I knew you were going to say that."

****

Veronica's neck and back screamed at her, and she was so tired she could barely sit up straight. "I should get some rest," she told herself, knowing if she didn't, tonight at work would be hell.

Instead of listening, she gave into the need to continue the search just a few more minutes. After all, she had no idea if, or when, the Guardians would figure out what she was doing and stop her. If she could find out something, she'd get the information to Joe as soon as she could. Just in case the Guardians took her away or something.

What *did* the Guardians do with vampires who didn't follow the rules? Nobody she'd ever talked to knew. The only thing everybody seemed to be in agreement about was that you didn't mess with the Guardians.

Ten minutes later, she clicked a link and a face she knew popped up on the screen: Spencer Drake. The brother of Ethan Drake—and a Guardian. She looked carefully at his info, seeing if anything made sense.

The answer popped into her head. The file code ended with Spencer's birth date. Okay, that was helpful information. The profiles she'd seen didn't include birthdates, so she wouldn't have figured it out if she hadn't happened to know Spencer's.

Okay, so she'd broken part of the code. She searched through Spencer's profile to see if she could find any other hints. Then she saw a code that looked familiar. Pulling her printed list close, she scanned the codes. Yes! She'd found a match. In seconds, a DNA profile that had to be Spencer's popped up on her screen.

Okay, but if she had to search through all the files it could take years. She tried an automated search, but it wouldn't work. The files must be locked in some way to prevent exactly what she was trying to do. In a last ditch effort, she decided to compare all the numbers to find some connection. It took her almost two hours, but finally she figured out the link between the codes.

It took some headache-inducing work to link birthdates and year of joining the Guardians, place of birth, and male or female, but eventually she got some parameters. She still had to go one file at a time, but at least she'd narrowed down the field.

She was just about to decide she would have to either skip work or stop digging until morning, when a photo came up that shocked her to her toenails. He couldn't be a Guardian. She'd have known, wouldn't she? After all they'd worked together for almost two years.

Pushing all that aside, she checked his DNA code to see if it related somehow to the other codes in the files, only to get an even bigger shock. The code on the profile, and the one of the killer matched.

Her breath caught in her throat. Todd Kennedy was Justin's killer.

****

"Hello, Mr. Burns, my name is Joe Sullivan. I wonder if you might be able to help me out."

Burns narrowed his eyes as he studied Joe. "You're not kin to Roark and Dawn Sullivan who own Mariner's Fish Fry are you?"

"Not that I know of, sir."

"They have some excellent blueberry pie. You should try a slice."

"I'll do that, sir. Do you happen to know a man named Kennedy? His first initial is T."

"Well, let me see," the old man said as he scratched his white beard and thought for a time. "I believe I do know of a Kennedy. Don't know his first name though. He's from someplace away. Hadn't seen him around much." Burns leaned closer to Joe. "He's not very friendly."

"Do you have any idea where he lives?" Joe asked, trying hard not to tell the old man to hurry.

"Nope, but I tell ya, I believe he's one of the science folks. We get a lot of them around here."

"Do you have any idea where he works?"

The old man thought for a long minute. "Nope. Some science place, I'd imagine. There's a few of 'em 'round here."

"Anything else you can tell us about him?"

Again the beard scratching and thinking. "Can't say as I can."

"Thank you, sir. You've been a big help." Joe shook the man's hand.

"You be careful, son. There's something going that's not right."

"What do you mean?"

"Don't rightly know. It's just that I've been around a while and know a few things. And I know something's going and it don't feel right."

"Thank you."

Mike shook the man's hand, then he and Joe headed out. "I guess we need to make phone calls.

Joe nodded. "Sounds like. Want to split the work fifty-fifty?"

"Sure."

They made a list of the nearby labs and any businesses likely to have a scientist on staff, split the list, and began calling. Excitement rose in Joe's chest. They were close. He just knew it.

****

Veronica tried to call Joe's cell, but once again the call went straight to voicemail. "Damn," she muttered. She read over the email she'd just written and sat back to consider. In the email she had admitted what she'd done and what she found. The document could get her in big trouble, but it might just bring some justice to one dead human. Maybe. Killing a human, after all, wasn't an illegal act for a vampire. It was all she could think to do, though. Spencer was the only Guardian she trusted, and wondered if she was being smart to even send the information to him. If she didn't do anything, though, all her work would be in vain.

With a little prayer to whoever was up there, she added blind copies to Ethan's email, and an online based email account of her own before she clicked send.

She tried once more to call Joe. When she got his voicemail again, she texted him to call her ASAP, grabbed her car keys, and paced. The sun should be going down soon. Until then she was stuck. Without a full protective outfit, which, unlike her sister, she didn't have because it was a pain in the ass. She wasn't going anywhere.

Damn! She had to find Joe and let him know what she'd found. Something was wrong here, something she didn't understand. Something that could put Joe's life at risk.

****

Joe growled at his cell phone.

"Down boy."

Joe scowled across the Lobster Shack table toward Mike. "The damn battery's dead."

Mike put his own phone down. "It's getting a little late in the day to be calling labs and businesses anyway."

Joe rubbed his aching neck. "We've called just about every place a scientist was likely to work. Maybe that old guy was wrong."

"Which puts us back at nowhere."

"Thanks for your encouragement, buddy."

Mike smiled. "No problem."

Joe glanced at his watch. "Veronica should be up, she's a scientist, maybe she knows who the hell this guy is."

"You can use my phone."

He shook his head. "Nah, I'd rather talk to her in person anyway. Let's go back to Justin's place. I'll plug in my phone, and we can grab heavier clothes. It's already getting chilly. By the time the sun's down, it'll feel like the air's full of ice."

"Boy that's the truth."

They headed toward Joe's rental car.

****

Dressed in gloves, long sleeves, and a wide-brimmed hat, Veronica braved the last rays of the sun to knock on Joe's door. When there was no answer, fear tightened her throat, making it hard to breathe. After knocking one last time, she tried the doorknob, but the door was locked. She tried once again to call him, and the call once again went straight to voicemail. "Where could he be?" Anywhere, as she realized his car wasn't in the small gravel parking lot.

"Think," she whispered, "where would he have gone?" He was investigating his brother's murder. Where was that likely to lead him? Into town probably.

With no better idea, she turned and headed toward town. She kept to the areas with trees as much as possible, so she could use their shade to help protect her from the long, harsh rays of the slowly setting sun. She had plenty to worry about; she didn't want to add getting burned again to the list.

****

Joe squinted in the sunset as he unlocked the door to Justin's apartment. As soon as he was inside, he reached for the cord to plug in his cell, but stopped in mid-movement. "We don't have time to charge this thing, let's just head over to Veronica's."

Mike had gone straight for the coats. "Sounds like a plan."

Joe dropped the phone on the coffee table and took the jacket Mike handed him. The two of them jumped into Joe's rental car again and headed toward town. They'd just turned from Main Street onto Pine Avenue, when Joe caught sight of a familiar form.

"What are you doing?" Mike asked as he pulled the car into the empty funeral home parking lot.

"That's Conner over there." He pointed to a hooded figure standing between the funeral home and the Historical Society building.

"How can you tell?"

"Trust me, it's him." Joe got out and rushed off toward the man.

Letting out a huge groan. Mike slid out of the passenger side of the car and followed him.

"Conner," Joe kept his voice just loud enough so the man could hear him. "Is that you?"

The hooded figure turned. "Yes, it's me."

He caught up to Conner. "Can you tell me anything that might help me find my brother's killer?"

Conner sighed. "So you are still determined to do this."

"I have to, for my brother's sake." Joe swallowed. "I've come to believe that if I don't find the killer, he won't be caught."

The man was quiet for a moment. "You're right about that."

"How can you be so sure?" Mike asked, from his position behind Joe.

"Because Justin's killer was one of our kind."

"Whatever he is," Mike said, "We think his name is Kennedy."

"That would make sense," Conner said. "Todd Kennedy is vampire."

****

Kevin sat in the shadows on a small hill overlooking a dirt area near the back of a big church. He watched as the man dressed in a T-shirt and shorts, a man he knew to be a priest, threw the basketball toward a hoop attached to a pole. The ball took a long, curved path up and over, and dropped easily into the middle of the net.

The kids scattered around him cheered laughed and fist-bumped each other and the priest. "Way to go, Father Zack!" one of them yelled.

Eleven kids were playing ball with the priest, most of them about Kevin's age.

"I guess I'm not as old as you guys thought, huh?"

the priest said. "It's getting late. Why don't we call an end for tonight?"

There was a round of objections, but the priest only shook his head. "I'm quite sure you have homework. Now get on home." The man, who looked nothing like Kevin thought of as a priest, waved a hand in the direction of town. Still complaining, the kids headed out.

Chuckling, the priest turned and walked toward the church, which led him in front of where Kevin was sitting. He looked up. "You didn't want to play?"

The man had noticed him? Strange. Most people either didn't see him or ignored him. "Not really my thing," Kevin told him.

"We play most afternoons, if you change your mind."

I'd love to.

"Nah. Got more important shit to do."

He'd expected the dirty word would get a rise out of the priest, or maybe encourage him to leave. Instead, the man climbed the small hill and took a seat beside him.

"So what do you like to do?" the guy, who looked like Santa Claus in a tie-dyed T-shirt, asked.

Kevin kicked at the dirt. "Just stuff. You know."

"With your friends?"

What was with this guy? "I'm not Catholic."

The priest chuckled. "That's okay, I'm not a teenager."

"How do you know if somebody's evil?" Kevin shot his gaze into the distance so the priest wouldn't see how surprised he was that his mouth had taken off by itself to ask that question.

"Well," the priest said. "I don't believe anyone is completely good or evil. We all have the potential for both inside us. The choices we make are what's important."

"What if somebody tells you a group of…of people are all evil? Should you believe them?"

"What do you think, son?"

Kevin dropped his gaze to the ground. "I don't know."

The priest put a firm hand on his shoulder. "Would you like a soda? Or maybe something from Julie's Sweet Shop? It's right around the corner." He pointed.

It sounded so good he almost drooled. "Sorry, I gotta go."

"If you change your mind, you know where I'll be."

Kevin nodded. "Thank you."

The priest moved his hand, and Kevin made for the woods. Things were making less sense all the time.

****

The darkness was almost complete, allowing Veronica to remove the hat. She'd always thought of Lobster Cove as a small place, but today it seemed huge. Where in the world was Joe? Her heart beat hard against her chest, and her breath came in big hard gasps. What if the killer had gotten to him while she was asleep? What if she lost the man she loved?

That had her stopping cold. What the hell was that? She couldn't be in love with Joe. He was human. She didn't want to mate with a vampire male, but she had with a human. But then, it wasn't just sex that she craved with Joe. It was something much stronger, much more intimate.

She sat on a bench and dropped her head into her hands. She had obviously lost her mind. When a vampire bonded with another—not just a casual mating, but a commitment—the two of them became mentally connected. *Linked*. But a vampire couldn't *Link* with a human. It was impossible.

In the midst of her confusion, she realized something she had managed to ignore over the last few days, she sensed Joe. When they were together they could read each other's minds. When apart, she could feel his mental touch. A psychic conduit connected them.

All at once, she realized two things: Impossible or not, she and Joe were already *Linked*. And she could use that *Link* to find him.

She shot to her feet and headed in the direction the mental pull was strongest.

****

Joe stood in the shadows near the mansion where he knew Veronica's lab to be. They'd parked in a small nearby clearing so as not to alert anyone to their presence.

"Are you sure about this?" Mike asked from beside him.

"No, but I think it's a good bet that Veronica knows this guy."

"You sure you don't remember her number?"

"Sorry." Joe looked back toward town. "Besides, she's on her way."

Mike turned a glare on him. "Just how the bloody hell would you know that?"

Joe shrugged. "Not a clue. I just know she is."

"She's nuts and she's rubbed off on you."

He shrugged again. Mike could think what he wanted. Joe sure as hell didn't have an explanation for what was happening.

Footsteps caught Joe's attention. Somebody was coming his way, and it wasn't Veronica.

A man stepped toward them and stopped. "I thought I heard something over here."

Joe recognized him, he'd seen the guy come and go from the lab. He was vampire too, of that he was positive. "We're waiting for somebody."

The man narrowed his eyes as he smiled. "Yes, I've seen you waiting for Veronica before."

Alarms went off in Joe's head, as he remembered Veronica saying she was worried about being seen talking to him in the lab's parking lot. He forced a chuckle. "Actually, no. We're waiting for a guy who said he could tell us where a great tittie bar was."

"Yeah," Mike put in. "I'm looking forward to a little fun."

The man's laugh sent icy shivers down Joe's spine. Whoever this guy was, he didn't have good intentions.

"You're lying."

Joe opened his mouth to protest, but before he could, several men stepped out of the trees surrounding the road and parking lot.

"Well," one of the newcomers, a man Joe recognized, said as he walked over to them. "What do we have here?"

Mike stepped toward the man. "Vince, buddy, how're you doing?"

"*Vincent*," he growled. "My name is Vincent."

"Hey, whatever you want, Vincent." Mike backed away, hands up. "Sorry, just trying to be friendly."

Vincent walked up to Mike and got right in his face. "You are not my friend."

The vampire still stood in the same place, a small satisfied smile on his lips, an expression of hate in his eyes.

"What the hell is this?" Joe asked.

"What happens when you mess in things that don't concern you." The vampire's smile widened.

"You know I have no idea what you're talking about, right?"

"You should stick with your own kind."

Joe stared at the vampire. "Would you like to explain that statement?"

Vince took a step toward Joe. "You're friendly with one of those creatures. Did you know they drink human blood to survive?"

"Yes."

Vince's expression turned to disgust. "Then how can you have anything to do with them? They're demons, I tell you. They're out to destroy mankind." His voice increased in intensity until at the end he was red-faced and all but shouting.

Joe just watched him. "Like the guy standing next to you?"

Vincent laughed. "Todd is just as human as you and me, but unlike you, he's dedicated to fighting the inhuman scum that threatens us."

Joe shrugged. No use trying to convince a crazy guy. And there was no doubt Vince was insane. "Whatever you say."

"You should take them to headquarters," Todd the vampire, said to the guy who hated vampires.

"Aren't you going too?" Joe asked.

"I have work to do."

"He's trying to find a cure," one of the other men said.

Vince spun and punched the guy so hard he fell on the ground. "You keep your mouth shut."

Cure for what? Were these men from the conspiracy Justin was investigating? If they were, why didn't they realize Todd was a vampire? "So there's a disease of some kind?"

Vincent spun and stalked over to Joe. "None of your damn business, traitor."

"I'm a traitor, huh? To what?"

"To your own kind, you idiot." Vincent glared at him.

"Is someone sick?" Mike took a step toward Vincent. "Maybe I could help."

Vincent's lips curled into an ugly snarl. "The only sick's going to be the Devil's spawn. They think they can control us, but we're not about to sit still like cattle to the slaughter."

Joe shot a glance toward Todd, who was looking smug. What the hell? "What happened to Justin?"

Vincent got within an inch of his face. "I don't know who killed your brother, but they saved us the trouble."

He didn't even remember moving, but the next thing Joe knew his fist connected with Vincent's face. Vincent dropped, and Joe stood over him. "Bastard."

Vincent just grinned. "You'd have to ask my momma about that."

"Go to hell." Joe tried to shake loose the two men who held him, but it was no use.

"Kinda trying to keep us all *out* of the hot place."

Vincent got to his feet. "Let's take them back to H.Q."

"I don't think so."

Joe looked toward the familiar voice to see Veronica standing to one side, her arm around the neck of one of the men. He mentally calculated everybody's position. This was about to get interesting.

All at once, Todd appeared behind her. Her eyes opened wide for a second, then closed. She dropped to the ground.

"We're screwed," Mike said.

Joe agreed.

Chapter 9

Kevin crouched in the shadows and watched as Vincent smarted off to the brother of the guy that got killed. He was sure Vincent would smack him around if he knew, but he kinda understood the guy. He was just trying to find out who killed his brother. Kevin figured if he had a brother who got killed, he'd want to know who did it.

The thing that really got him, though, was that nobody seemed to realize that Todd guy was one of the creatures. Kevin wasn't sure how he knew, he just did. Was the man a spy? He needed to let Vincent know, if Vincent would even believe him.

He saw the crazy woman behind Lucas, but she moved so fast he didn't have time to shout a warning before she caught Lucas and held him with an arm around his throat.

He stood to go help his fellow Alliance of True Humanity members, then thought better of the idea. If he went to help them, he'd be in the same position they were. If he stayed where he was, maybe he could figure out what to do.

The thing was, something wasn't right. Todd was one of those creature things, but Vince didn't know it. He should do something, help them out, warn them about Todd. They would just laugh at him though. Say he was a kid, like they always did.

Then the Todd guy did something to the crazy woman, knocking her out. It was odd but Kevin wanted to help her more than he wanted to help his fellow Alliance members. He couldn't do that though, he had to be loyal to his friends. After all, he owed Vincent a lot.

Didn't he?

****

Veronica woke in a dark dank room that smelled of dust and animal droppings. Just enough moonlight came through the single window to allow her to ascertain the place was approximately three meters by four meters. Her head hurt and she couldn't remember how she got in that nasty place. What the hell happened? Oh yeah, she was rescuing Joe.

She pushed herself to a sitting position, not easy with bound hands and feet. Her head pounded with the effort, and she fought back nausea. Memory flashes blew by of holding that human by the throat and thinking she had things under control.

With a groan, she remembered Todd coming up behind her, then a stinging sensation in her neck. She reached up and touched the area, which was sore to the touch. Just as she thought, he'd drugged her with something. She vowed to get even with him, just as soon as she got out of there and found Joe. He was somewhere nearby. She could feel him.

Her heart twisted at the thought of what these insane humans might do to him. She had to get going. Though it shot knives through her head and twisted her stomach, she pulled at the restraints on her hands.

Nothing happened.

Well, that was strange. Was the problem that she

was still weak from whatever that son-of-an-amoeba gave her? She pulled at the metal again without result. Maybe she could release herself some other way. She held up her hands and squinted through the darkness.

Handcuffs. Okay, she'd already surmised that. Shouldn't be a problem for her. She gave the cuffs an experimental pull in both directions. There was no give at all in the metal. Something was wrong here.

Bringing the cuffs to her mouth, she touched her tongue to the metal. Steel. She pulled on it again. It couldn't be. How would a small group of misguided, uninformed humans get their hands on something with a tensile strength greater than Maraging steel—which she should at least be able to bend? The only alternative was that she was still weak enough from the drug she couldn't bend or break a frigging pair of handcuffs, and she didn't believe that for a minute.

She wiggled her legs, and verified what she suspected; her ankles were also bound with handcuffs. A couple of hard jerks with her legs got her nowhere, so she leaned forward. The handcuffs that bound her ankles seemed to be made of the same unbreakable material as those binding her hands. Pulling with the combined strength of both hands and legs got her nowhere, and she had to accept the idea that she wasn't likely to get free with brute strength. Her heart sank as she thought about Joe and his friend. Were they near?

Closing her eyes, she pictured Joe's handsome face and let her ability slide out to reach for him. Seconds later, she caught his mind. She couldn't read his thoughts, but she got that he was bound in a dark room just like her. He was close, but not in an adjoining room. Close enough, though, to get to him in a hurry, if she could just escape those hideous handcuffs.

The sound of footsteps warned her, and she leaned back and closed her eyes so she would seem to still be drugged.

The door opened and a figure slipped quietly into the room. "Are you awake, crazy woman?"

She recognized the voice of the boy who'd tried to rob her, the one she'd taken blood from, the one who'd attacked Joe. "Yes."

"Who are you?" he asked.

"My name is Veronica.

"Your whole name."

"Okay, it's Veronica Teal, Ph.D. I work as a biochemist."

"At a lab in that big old Seabird house."

She licked her lips. What the hell, he already knew about it. "Yes."

He moved closer and she could see an outline of his face. He looked so young, she had a strong desire to hold him and tell him everything would be all right. "You're one of those creatures Vincent hates, aren't you?"

"Yes, I believe so."

"What *are* you?" He moved a little closer, tilted his head to one side, and leaned in like he was trying to figure out what he was seeing.

"I'm vampire."

He blinked, but stood his ground. "Does that mean vampire like in horror novels?"

"Not exactly, but the term is fairly accurate."

"Then why did you try to help those humans?"

"Because they're my friends."

Even in the dim light she could see the confusion

on his face. "You're friends with humans?"

"Yes, most of my friends are human," she admitted, to him and to herself.

"That doesn't make sense. Humans and your kind hate each other."

She swallowed, how did she explain something so complicated in a few sentences. "Actually, there isn't much difference between you and me."

"You're lying."

"No, I'm not. My job is genetics. I know a lot about the basic differences between humans and vampires. There is less difference in our genetic codes than between a chimpanzee and a human. Quite a lot less."

"I read that humans and chimps are related, but I didn't understand." He moved toward her again, and she could feel his curiosity.

"What do you know about genes and DNA?"

He shrugged. "I know that DNA makes genes, and genes are like the blueprint for a person."

Veronica smiled. This kid was too smart to be hustling for survival. "That's right. And the difference between human genes and vampire genes is very small."

He tilted his head to one side. "Are you vampire people making a virus to wipe us out?"

Shocked, she leaned back so hard she hit her head on the wall. "Why would we do that?"

"Vincent says you want to kill a bunch of us so you could manage us better."

"That doesn't make sense. Humans run the world. You control the businesses, industries, and services. Without humans, civilization would collapse. Nobody wants that."

He propped against what looked like a box. "Couldn't the vampires run things?"

"There aren't nearly enough of us for that, even if we knew how." She tried to catch his gaze. "What's your name?"

"Kevin."

"Kevin, I don't mean you any harm."

"You wanted to help me, didn't you? When I tried to mug you."

He remembered? Odd. "Yes, I didn't want you to live on the streets and steal for survival. I still don't."

"Why do you care? You aren't even human."

"Because you're young, and you deserve better than to be manipulated by anybody who helps you out."

He stared at her for a long time; so long she was afraid she'd gone too far.

Finally, he spoke. "I can't go home. There's nothing back home but a drunk father who only cares about winning big. Trouble is, he always loses. And takes it out on me."

Her heart bled when she heard the words. His face twisted, and because of her psychic ability, she experienced his painful memory along with him. "Is there someplace else you could go?"

The sound of footsteps had Kevin sucking in his breath. "They can't find me here."

****

Joe struggled against his restraints, but all he was doing was making his wrists and ankles sore. There had to be a way to pull loose or slide out of the handcuffs, but he wasn't finding any. With his ankles handcuffed, even if he managed to get to his feet, he couldn't walk.

There had to be some way, though. The dark, damp, nasty smelling room was the last place he wanted to be, and he was determined to get loose ASAP.

Beside him, Mike let out a long creative stream of four letter words. Laughing in spite of himself, Joe looked toward his friend. "A little frustrated, are we?"

"Shut the hell up, smartass."

Joe only laughed again. "What bothers you the most, being restrained, the germs in here that are multiplying exponentially as we speak, or the possibility that your precious surgeon's hands might be damaged?"

"Why do I consider you a friend?"

"Because of my charming personality."

Another long, creative blast of profanity came from Mike, and Joe laughed. His amusement didn't last long, though. He was too worried about getting away from this band of fanatical shitheads. "I'm sorry I ever doubted you, Justin," he murmured.

He heard footsteps just before the door swung open. In the dim light Vincent's outline was just visible as it came toward him.

Vincent stopped just far enough that Joe couldn't nail him with his restrained legs. "What is it with you and your nosy brother?"

Joe glared into the man's face as he jerked at his restraints. "Why did you kill Justin?"

Vincent squatted in front of him. "I told you before. we had nothing to do with your brother's death."

Joe put all his anger and frustration in to breaking the handcuffs so he could choke the life out of this asshole. "You're a lying piece of shit!"

Vincent only smiled. "I may or may not be excrement, but I'm not lying. I honestly have no idea who killed him, but, like I said, whoever it was did our organization a favor."

Joe slid his legs under him, and struggled to get to his feet. He heard Mike yell a warning just before something hard hit him in the back of the head. As he dropped to the floor, he heard Mike's tirade against their captors. Then everything went black.

****

When Todd walked in, Veronica instinctually sent out a strong mental prod, but hit an impenetrable barrier.

He grinned. "You can't do that to me, I'm a Guardian." His expression hardened. "Or at least I used to be. Arrogant pricks and their antiquated rules."

"What do you think you're doing?" she asked.

He smiled again. "What those idiots who supposedly guard us are afraid to do." He turned and looked toward the corner where Kevin was hiding. "Come on out, human. I know you're there."

"It's okay, Kevin," she said, hoping she sounded more sure than she was.

Slowly Kevin moved from behind a wooden box. "Who are you?"

Todd grinned. "I'm your worst nightmare, kid."

"Stop it!" Veronica snapped. "Don't pay any attention to him, Kevin. He's a jerk."

Todd turned to her. "Jerk, huh? Is that why you rejected my approaches?"

"That would be it."

He laughed. "So you turned to a human for your biological needs. Traded down, I'd say."

"You'd be wrong. Joe's a far better man than you'll ever be."

"That has to be the craziest thing I've ever heard. It's not possible for a human to be superior to a vampire."

Veronica smiled. "I beg to differ. Most humans are superior to you."

The slap knocked her onto her side. She spat the nasty dirt out of her mouth and pushed herself back to a sitting position. "Jealous, Todd?"

Todd threw back his head and laughed heartily. "Of a human? You're delusional, Dr. Teal."

Kevin took a step toward him. "Leave Dr. Veronica alone! She's nice, and she cares about people. She's smart too, and she knows all about genes and DNA and the differences between my people and yours."

"Thank you, Kevin." Tears burned Veronica's eyes as she smiled toward Kevin. She would find a way to get him out of this craziness and help him find a good life. Of course, she had to get herself out of this mess first.

"So you have a little trained human. How cute."

"Why are you hanging out with a bunch of humans who hate vampires? It makes no sense."

"Sure it does. If they think I'm one of them, I can manipulate the situation to my liking."

Fear slithered its way through her. "And what would your 'liking' be?"

His lips pulled into a huge, arrogant smile. "Taking advantage of a wonderful opportunity. Vincent knows we aren't developing a virus to kill humans. He wants to develop a virus to kill vampires."

Okay, maybe it wasn't as bad as it seemed. "So you're making sure that virus never happens."

He snorted. "What fun would that be? No, I'm making sure it happens."

Her breath sucked in so hard it hurt. "Why?"

"Because some vampires are damn near impossible to kill."

All at once the pieces fell into place. "You want to destroy the Guardians."

"Very good, little girl." He waved his hand in a dismissing motion. "The Guardians are no longer protecting our kind. they have become a quivering mass of old men following the humans and their 'political correctness' down the path to hell."

"And you believe you're the person to stop them."

He put a hand on his chest as he smiled. "I do possess the needed skills, after all."

"And just what skills do you believe are needed?"

"Let's see, knowledge of vampire anatomy, knowledge of how the Guardians operate, the knowledge and ability to manipulate viruses, access to a lab—"

"You used our lab to work with deadly viruses!" She forced herself to her feet, while she pulled so hard against her restraints blood ran over her hand. "You are either the stupidest person to ever live, or the most arrogant. How dare you subject everybody working at our Lab to a deadly virus that you aren't even taking proper precautions to contain! You could kill us all and let loose a plague capable of killing every single vampire on earth!"

He looked at her with an expression of pure loathing. "Calm down, Veronica. You're going to hurt yourself."

Out of the corner of her eye, she saw Kevin edging toward the door. She focused all her rage on Todd—and she had an abundance of it. "I'm going to kill you, slowly and painfully and I'm going to enjoy every second of it."

"Good luck with that." He spun to pin Kevin with a glare. "You didn't really think you could get away from me, did you?"

"Run!" she yelled, then immediately shot every bit of her mental ability at Todd. Reaching inside herself for every tiny bit of strength she had, she pounded the arrogant maniac with it. She pushed so hard something in her eye popped, and what was probably blood ran down her face. She didn't stop though. If she could kill this thing Todd had become, she would be happy to do just that.

All at once he threw power back at her so hard she stumbled backward. She focused on continuing the attack, but all her strength was gone. She hit the floor hard just before everything went black.

Chapter 10

His head would explode, Joe was sure of it. Groaning, he shoved himself over on his side, then up into a sitting position.

"Thank God you're awake. I was getting worried."

Joe looked at where Mike was sitting beside him. "How long was I out?"

"Long enough for your friend the doctor to diagnose a concussion."

Joe aimed a derisive look at him. "Glad that you were here to make that diagnosis."

Mike dipped his head. "Glad I could be of service."

He brought his hands up so he could rub his aching forehead. "Did anything happen while I was having this concussion?"

"Nope. Vince the snake hit you, then he and his minions left." Mike shook his head. "He's insane, you know."

Joe glanced at him from under his hands. "No shit, Sherlock. It doesn't take a freaking MD to diagnose that one."

"Ha-ha, you're such a comedian."

Joe hit him with a glare, then turned his attention to testing his handcuffs again. It seemed to him it was slightly lighter outside. Moonlight or beginning sunrise? If the sun rose, Veronica could be in serious danger. He knew she was close, but the link seemed quiet. Too quiet. Was she asleep? Focused on something—like getting out? Unconscious? Something was wrong, and, he didn't like it. "We have to get out of here."

Mike gave him a glare that should have shoved him backwards. "No shit, Sherlock. While you were having your beauty sleep, I've been trying to figure out an escape plan."

"Come up with anything?"

"Actually, I've been thinking if I could find a long, small piece of metal, I might be able to pick the lock on the cuffs."

Joe stared at his friend for a moment, then smiled as memories wafted back to him. "You used to be good at that stuff."

"It's been forever since I've done any lock picking, but I think I might remember how."

"We ain't got a lot to lose here, buddy."

Mike nodded slowly. "Exactly what I was thinking. Now if we could just find something long enough and thin enough to get into the lock."

They fumbled in the dark for so long Joe broke out in a sweat. "Damn Maine. Too hot, or too cold."

"Get over it, Goldilocks."

The sound of footsteps hurrying toward them kept him from replying. Instead, he rushed to try to get back in the position he'd been left in. Beside him, Mike was doing the same thing.

The kid who'd attacked him rushed in. Joe tensed for a repeat fight, but the kid stopped near them, leaned against the wall, and stood gasping for breath. "We have to help Veronica," he gasped, and Joe realized his face was bright red.

"What happened?"

"She helped me get away and that Todd guy knocked her down without touching her. We have to rescue her and get out of here."

Joe studied the teenager. "She helped you get away? You expect me to believe that after you attacked me and could have hurt her badly in the process."

The boy groaned. "Look, I don't blame you for not believing me, but I'm not dumb. I talked to her a long time. She's nice."

"I'm not buying it, kid."

He straightened his back and glared at Joe. "Kevin. My name is Kevin, and I don't care what you think about me. You have to help me get Veronica out of here. I can't do it myself, not with that vampire guy around. He's like a Terminator or some shit."

Joe thought for a minute, then nodded. "Okay, let's say we agree to help you. We have a little snag." He held up his cuffed hands.

"No problem, man. I've got the key." Kevin held up the small shiny treasure.

"Well what are you waiting for? Let's get the hell out of here."

Kevin grinned. "Finally, we get to kick some ass!"

****

Veronica woke with either another headache or the same one but worse, she wasn't sure which. When she flexed her left arm, she felt a sharp ache just below the shoulder. She groaned and forced herself to sit.

Todd smiled at her. He sat on a box a few meters from her. "Sleeping Beauty awakens."

"Go to hell."

He laughed. "I can't believe someone with your

intelligence would buy in to a human superstitious belief."

"I knew you were a jerk, I just didn't know you were evil."

He crossed his legs and leaned back against another box behind him. "And yet another human superstitious belief."

"No, they're right about evil. I see it in your eyes." She rotated her shoulder, but it only made the ache worse.

"I'm afraid the injection site might ache for a bit, but it should stop soon."

Icy fear shot through her veins. "What did you do?"

He leaned toward her, resting his forearms on his knees. "We need a test subject, and you're the most logical choice."

"Oh my God! You didn't. You couldn't."

"Hmm, God is an interesting topic Perhaps we will have enough time to debate the subject before you succumb to the virus."

Her breath came in short, hard exhalations as hot anger blew through her body. "How dare you."

He shrugged. "You got yourself into this by running with those nasty human animals."

"Like you do?"

"No, I use them for my own benefit. That, Dr. Teal, is what humans are for."

"They are only a few genes different from us."

"Yes, and a world apart." He leaned forward. "I wish you had allowed me to mate with you. We could have enjoyed ourselves while I ruled over this world."

He touched her cheek, and she used her cuffed

hands to shove his away.

"Odd," he said. "Even knowing that you gave yourself to that human scum, I believe I'd mate with you if you allowed me."

"Too late, idiot. You killed me, remember."

"Oh that," he scoffed. "You don't think I'd have something that dangerous around without making a cure, do you?"

"Of course not." She'd suspected, now she knew he had a cure. She had to figure a way out of this mess. She wasn't about to give up. Not when she sensed Joe nearby.

The sound of a scuffle outside caught Todd's attention. He listened for a moment, then stood and went toward the door. "What the hell are those idiotic humans doing now?"

"Coming to burn you at the stake."

"You are such a charming woman," he told her.

She kept her gaze on him and reached out with her mental ability. All she had to do was distract him.

"What do you think you're doing?" he asked. He shoved back at her mentally, but by that time Joe was behind him and a big piece of wood came down on Todd's head.

Joe ran to her. "Are you all right? There's blood under your eye."

"Broken blood vessel. Sometimes happens with vampires when we push our psychic abilities too hard. I'm fine.

He didn't look convinced as he cupped her cheeks and gently wiped the dried blood away with his thumb. The touch of his hands on her face had her stomach dancing with pleasure. She wanted him to hold her forever. Then his lips touched hers, and she forgot everything for a blissful moment.

A movement behind Joe jerked her out of the bliss. "Look out," she said, as she thrust a mental spear at Todd.

Joe drove an elbow into the vampire's middle, then stood to continue the fight.

Veronica felt something in her hand and looked down. Her fear eased when she realized what she had. While she continued sending quick, distracting mental pokes at Todd, she struggled to use the key Joe had given her to unlock her handcuffs.

****

Joe ducked yet another punch coming at him faster than should be possible. He knew he'd never have managed to keep up his end of this fight if Veronica wasn't doing some kind of mental kung fu with Todd.

That and his determination to bring his brother's killer to justice was all he had going for him. He just hoped it would be enough.

Todd threw a punch that connected with Joe's right shoulder. "Good thing I'm left-handed." He nailed the vampire with a punch to his chin.

Todd barely reacted to the blow. Joe braced for another barrage, but then Veronica appeared behind Todd. She grabbed the man and shoved him toward the wall. Before Joe could react, Todd swung back around and hit Veronica. She stumbled backward into a streak of early morning sunlight shining through a space between two boards. Gasping, she jerked away from the deadly rays and back into the darkness of the room.

Molten rage erupted within Joe. Oblivious to the danger, he charged Todd, grabbed him, and tossed him toward the door. He only managed to move the vampire a few feet.

Determined to hurt the man, Joe put his head down and charged toward Todd with everything he had. Todd expected him this time, and Joe only moved him a few inches.

It was enough for Veronica to take advantage of, and one long leg kicked Todd against the door. He bounced off, but a thin line of sun came through the door. Joe ran toward Todd, and the vampire smiled waiting for the next round.

At the last second, Joe turned for the door and threw his weight against it. Sunlight blew through the room, and Todd instinctively threw up his arm. Joe, adrenaline pumping through his veins, grabbed the distracted Todd and threw him through the opening into the dirt outside. Todd howled long and hard.

Joe went to Veronica, making sure to keep an eye toward his opponent. "Are you okay, sweetheart?"

"You can't let him die."

He stared at her. "Why the hell not?"

"He gave me the virus, and he's the only one who knows where the cure is."

An icy wave of fear washed over him. "What virus?"

Tears glistened in her eyes. "The one he was really developing. A virus designed to kill vampires."

Joe all but flew out the door and jerked Todd back into the dark building. "Where's the cure for what you gave Veronica?"

The man's face bubbled and oozed with blisters, but he didn't show pain as his lips pulled into a twisted smile. "Wouldn't you like to know?"

"If you don't tell me, I'm going to put you back out in the sun."

Todd shrugged. "I prefer that to being hounded in a Guardian prison for the rest of my life."

"You're insane."

"Maybe, but I'm also a genius. Even a gnat human like you has to admit that."

Veronica had come around Joe and was sitting on her heels near Todd's head, her eyes closed. "Where is it, Todd?" she asked.

"You can poke in my head all you want. I have Guardian training. You'll never find where I hid it."

She looked at Joe. "He's telling the truth. I can't push past a Guardian's defenses."

He held her gaze. "Not by yourself."

She blinked. "I don't think that's possible."

"Honey, not that long ago, I didn't think you were possible."

Her soft laugh sent tingles through his body. "I know the feeling," she whispered, as she took his hand in hers.

What happened next was the wildest thing Joe had ever experienced. He would have thought it impossible, but he was in her thoughts, her feelings, her memories. Everything swirled and tangled, moving through his thoughts and making him feel he was in the middle of a kaleidoscope. He was part of her colorful and amazing life as it whizzed by.

"Joe," Veronica's voice echoed in his head. "This way."

He had no idea how he did it, but he followed her as she moved through the swirl. He was disoriented for a moment, his head swimming with something akin to vertigo. When the feeling cleared, he saw his life simultaneously through her eyes and his own. His senses reeled with the sensation, and all he could do was follow Veronica's lead.

And then they were in Todd's head.

Seconds later they moved through an area that was dark, seemingly without even a tiny splinter of light. He wondered how he could see, and almost wished he couldn't. The area was cold and creepy; and the smell was horrible. It was like walking through a swamp of pus.

Then they were in front of a wall. He put out his hand and pushed against the barrier. It gave a little, like it was clay.

"We have to get through," she said.

"Let's do it."

They pushed simultaneously, and slowly, one inch at a time, the barrier caved in on itself until they were able to walk through the thin remainder.

They were in an odd version of a lab. Everything swirled and twisted, and one area was twice as large as the rest of the place. "Todd's workstation," she told him, though he'd already figured that out.

"He thinks he's hot shit."

Her laugh echoed in his head. "That he does."

At first Joe tried to be careful with the equipment, but then he realized this was just a representation within Todd's mind, and he gave up on careful and went to fast and furious. "How long do we have to get this stuff for you?" he asked.

"I'm not sure," she said, "but I'd guess twelve to twenty-four hours before the infection becomes critical."

Just a few hours to get this bastard's cure. They'd better find it, and it had damn well better do what it was supposed to. He'd only just found her, he wasn't about to lose the woman he loved.

Love? The word quivered as if it sat on the string of a bow just after the arrow left it. He turned to see Veronica staring at him; the wary question was coming from her.

"I love you," he said.

The lab twisted, knocking them around like feathers in a tornado.

"He's fighting us," she yelled.

He put everything he could into forcing the lab back into its original shape, but everything continued to swirl and twist. Dark purple, then black seeped into the place where the lab was, and the air around Joe thickened.

"We have to leave," Veronica said.

"Not yet, we can still fight him."

"We can't," she said. "He was trained as a Guardian. We were lucky to get as much as we did.

She appeared beside him and took his hand in hers. "Let's go."

Reality took shape around him, and Veronica looked into his eyes. "I love you too," she whispered.

The laugh tore Joe from the sweet moment, and he looked down at the blackened, oozing shell of a man lying beside them. A human would be dead.

"Aren't you two sweet," Todd croaked. "Sick, disgusting, freaks that you are."

"We love you too." Mike's voice came from behind them.

Joe turned to see Mike, Kevin, and Conner.

"Conner?"

"I suspected you might need help, so I followed the emotional trail."

"He showed up and helped us with the humans," Mike said. "You two all right?"

Joe looked into Veronica's beautiful green eyes and shook his head. "No, we have to get to the lab. Now. That bastard gave Veronica some kind of deadly virus."

"My car is nearby." Conner looked at Veronica. "The windows are treated, and I have another coat, gloves, and hat in my trunk.

"Thank you, Conner."

The required garments were brought in and soon the group headed toward Conner's car.

When Veronica took his arm, Joe saw the pallor and fatigue in her features. The reality of the situation hit him like a hard punch.

He put his arm around her as they walked. He would find that damn antidote if it was the last thing he did. He'd just found the woman he wanted to spend the rest of his life with, he wasn't about to let her die. No matter what it cost him.

Chapter 11

Veronica fought the weakness that pulled at her as if gravity had increased threefold. It took all her strength to continue searching the lab. It seemed she'd been looking through drawers and cabinets for hours, but she knew it had only been a few minutes.

"What exactly are we looking for?" Conner asked.

"Maybe a capped vial," Veronica said. "A small bottle with an odd label. Anything that looks out of place."

"That's everything," Conner said. "At least to me."

"How about an asthma inhaler?" Kevin said. "They did that on *Criminal Minds* once."

Veronica leaned a hand against the nearest counter and put the other to her aching head. "Sure, it could be just about anything or anywhere."

"We'll find it," Joe's reassuring voice warmed her, but she could feel the doubt inside him.

"What in blazes is going on here?"

Veronica turned to see Dr. Wright staring at them, red-faced, fists clenched, and ready to protect his lab at all costs. "Sir, they're helping me."

"Helping you what? These are *humans*, Dr. Teal."

Forcing her aching head to focus took a lot, but somehow she managed. "Sir, Todd was working on his own project. He developed a virus and—"

"His own project? What are you talking about?"

She took a deep breath and tried to steady her shaking body. "Todd was working on a virus that kills vampires."

Dr. Wright laughed. "That's the most ridiculous thing I've ever heard. Why in the world would he do that? Mutating a virus so that it kills our kind could change the entire balance of power between the human population and ours."

She swallowed. "Sir, I don't think Todd is entirely sane."

"No shit, Sherlock." Somebody, she thought it was Mike, muttered behind her. She fought the threatening smile and kept her gaze on Dr. Wright's.

"How can you say that? Dr. Kennedy is an excellent researcher. And what are you looking for here?"

"He used the resources of this lab to develop the virus."

The man's eyes widened. "This lab isn't equipped for viral research."

She stared into his face. "Exactly."

"Why would he do something so reckless?"

"To kill off vampires he doesn't like. Mostly the Guardians."

"That still doesn't explain why you've brought others into this facility. Dr. Wright's confused expression added frustration to her growing fatigue.

She thrust her left shoulder in his face and pointed to the red spot. "He injected me with the virus, and if we don't find the treatment soon, I'm going to die."

Dr. Wright stepped back and waved his arms. "This is a fantasy designed to confuse me so that you can take whatever it was you missed the first time you broke in here. Well, it won't work. I've already called the Guardians."

"She's telling the truth." The deep voice carried an edge that could only come from one source: a Guardian.

Dr. Wright turned. "Surely you don't believe her?"

"Actually, yes, I do."

Welcome relief washed over her. "Spencer."

He came closer and put a hand on her shoulder. "Any idea what kind of virus he gave you?"

"No, and the rest of you, especially the vampires, should probably get out. The virus might become contagious."

"Excellent idea." Dr. Wright exited, his expression telling her he believed none of it, his brisk steps saying he wasn't taking any chances.

"I'm not going anywhere," Joe said from behind her.

"Me either," Spencer Drake said, giving her shoulder a quick squeeze as if to confirm the statement.

Mike and Conner echoed the desire to help. Kevin ignored them all as he continued to search the lab.

"Let's get busy then." She turned and almost tripped. Joe caught her and walked with her to Todd's office.

Joe ransacked file cabinets and bookcases. She sat in the desk chair and methodically pulled out drawers and looked in nooks and crevices. It only took a couple of minutes to discover one drawer of Todd's desk was locked, and she didn't see the key anywhere. For a second, guilt twisted her heart. Then she remembered the kind of man Todd was. She grabbed the drawer and jerked. Nothing happened.

"Hey, Mike," Joe yelled out the office door, "we

could use some of your special skill in here."

Veronica pulled hard at the desk drawer. What the hell was it with all this super-strong metal today?

"Allow me," Mike said, sitting on his heels beside her. He bent two paper clips, shoved them in the lock, did some sort of twisting thing—and the drawer opened

"So you can pick locks?"

"Just one of my many talents." Mike looked at her for a moment, frowned, and raised a hand to her forehead. "Your temp is elevated."

She closed her eyes for a moment. "We might not find it in time."

"Bullshit. We'll find it in plenty of time." Joe took Mike's place beside her, while Mike slipped out the door.

"We have to be realistic."

"Okay, it's realistic that you're going to be fine and we're going to spend many happy years together."

"I hope you're right."

"I am." He gently kissed her before he went back to the file cabinets.

It wouldn't make sense to keep the cure in a locked drawer. It would be way too obvious. Right? But then, Todd was arrogant. And locking something up was logical.

Shaking the thoughts out of her head she took everything out of the drawer one piece at a time. The search seemed to take forever, and she wasn't sure how much longer she could keep going.

Mike poked his head in the door. "I found notes, but it would take several hours to make the serum."

Joe looked her way. "We don't have that kind of time."

"So it's a liquid?" She asked.

"Yes," Mike said. "It's an injectable serum."

"We have to keep searching," Joe said.

Veronica looked down at the desk. Where would you put something as valuable as that cure? For all Todd knew, he might have to use it on himself one day. He'd have it handy, but hidden.

Then it dawned on her. Didn't the bottom drawer seem too shallow? She shoved it in a bit, so she could see the outside. It was definitely smaller than the front would suggest. Afraid to even consider that she might have found the answer, she jerked the remainder of the contents out of the drawer and ran her hand around, feeling for a loose place, or hook, or latch, or something.

The bottom shifted when she touched the back right corner, and she gave it an experimental push. The false bottom of the drawer tipped up in the front.

Joe and Mike had come over and stood near her. She glanced up at Joe, and he gave her an encouraging smile.

Holding the corner down with one hand, she slipped her fingers under the front of the piece that had flipped up. The entire false bottom came out in her hands, revealing vials and syringes. She'd found the cure. Now if there was time to use it.

****

As Veronica moved the false drawer aside to reveal what must be the cure, Joe let out a breath he hadn't realized he was holding. Relief all but knocked him to the floor.

"He was even nice enough to leave directions," Mike said, holding up a neatly penned sheet of paper.

"Would you feel comfortable injecting me?" Veronica asked Mike. "I'm a coward with needles."

"I'd feel better if we did this in a hospital."

"They wouldn't understand my physiology, or a serum from a non-medical lab," she told him, and held out a vial and syringe. "Besides, there isn't time."

Mike nodded, and got to work getting things ready.

Joe sat on his heels beside her. "I'll be right here with you."

"Thank you." She squeezed his hand. "I'm glad you're here."

"I wouldn't be anywhere else."

"Okay, Veronica," Mike said. "It says intravenous."

She held out her arm. Do what you need to."

They found a piece of rubber tubing in the drawer, and Mike wrapped it around her upper arm. "He was prepared."

"Not for us," Joe said, and winked at Veronica.

Mike wiped her inner elbow with alcohol on a cotton ball. "Here we go."

Joe put his fingers on her chin and turned her to face him. "Look at me," he whispered.

She winced when he stuck the needle in her arm, and there was a moment of calm. Then she gasped and gripped his hand hard enough to hurt.

"I'm sorry, Veronica," Mike said. "It's been a while since I've done this."

"It's not you, the serum burns."

Joe gently rubbed her other arm and tried to send her calming energy. He had no idea what he was doing, but he had to try something. She gave him a shaky smile, and his heart flipped over.

"I'm done," Mike said. "I'll hold on to this for a minute."

"I have bandages in my desk drawer," she said.

"I'll get one," Joe kissed her cheek, then took off to the other office.

Once alone, he leaned a hand against Veronica's desk and allowed himself to confront the terror of the last few hours. He knew who Justin's killer was. He'd beaten the shit out of that maggot and thrust him into the burning sunlight. He should be relieved, but all he could think about was that he might still lose the woman he loved.

He took a deep breath, shoved his fear to the back of his mind, and pulled open the top drawer. Right now, Veronica needed him, and he had to be strong for her. He might have failed his brother, but he wouldn't fail the woman he hoped would agree to be his wife.

Chapter 12

Veronica lay on the couch in Dr. Wright's office and stared at the ceiling while her mind bounced between the certainty she would die, and thinking about what her future would be like with Joe.

Of course, she had no right to consider a life with him. Yes, he said he loved her, but that didn't mean he'd want to spend his life with a woman of a totally different species. A woman who drank the blood of his kind to survive.

If she didn't die from this damn virus.

A chill moved through her so hard her teeth chattered. Joe was at her side instantly, tucking her covers and feeling her forehead. "You're burning up. I'll get Mike."

In spite of the painful shivers, she must have dozed, because the next time she opened her eyes Mike was holding her wrist and looking at his watch. "Bad?" she was appalled at how weak and pathetic her voice sounded.

"Temp's high, pulse is fast, respirations rapid, consciousness in and out. Do you know who I am?"

"Not the man I want holding my hand." The smile took less effort that she'd have thought.

Mike smiled back and relinquished her hand to Joe, who she'd already spotted standing behind Mike. "How are you?" he asked.

"Tired."

"Just rest."

She gripped his hand. "I don't want to sleep if…if the cure…doesn't work…"

"Don't think that way, honey. Just rest and get well." He kissed her forehead. "I love you."

"I love you too." At least she thought she said the words before everything faded again.

****

Joe sat, watching Veronica sleep. She looked so peaceful, but he knew a battle raged inside her body. He sent up a silent prayer that she won that fight, then stood and pulled Mike aside. "Is she going to be okay?"

"I honestly don't know, Joe. We're dealing with an unknown virus, I don't know how her physiology works, the cure is untested, and we aren't even in a hospital where I could do tests."

"Would it help if she had some blood?"

Mike blinked. "I have no idea. That's part of that unknown physiology. Plus, I don't know what the virus is doing to her." He shook his head. "I really wish we were in a hospital."

A spike of anger rose in Joe. "Where they would have no idea what to do for her, and I doubt they'd let you give her a concoction mixed up in a small, private lab by a vengeful murderer." He glanced at Veronica. "And they sure as hell wouldn't let me feed her my blood."

Mike grasped his shoulder. "I'm sorry. I guess I'm just spoiled by having all kinds of equipment and supplies available. It's hard to get into the mode of an old country doctor who didn't have a lot to work with, and with gaps in his knowledge that had the potential to hurt."

Joe closed his eyes for a moment, then looked at his friend. "I'm scared."

"I know."

"No woman has ever stirred my feelings, my heart, the way she does. Ever."

"She's strong. She's got an excellent chance."

"I want more than that." Joe turned and walked into the lab, where the others were waiting.

"Is she okay," Kevin asked.

He nodded, noted the kid's expression of relief, and went over to where Conner and the Guardian dude were standing. "I need to ask something."

The Guardian, who Veronica had called Spencer, nodded. "What is it you need?"

"Would it help if she had some blood?"

Conner raised an eyebrow. "Are you volunteering?"

"Yes, of course," Joe told him. "I'll do whatever I can to help Veronica."

"You really care for her."

Joe looked into Spencer's eyes. "Yes, I do."

He seemed to study Joe for a moment before he spoke. "I'll make a couple of phone calls, see if I can find out if blood would be a good idea."

"Hurry."

"I will." The Guardian pulled out his cell as he turned away.

Joe went back to Veronica to hold her hand and wait. His watch told him it had only been a few minutes, his heart said hours were passing. Just when he thought he couldn't stand the waiting one more second, Veronica's hand tightened on his. Her eyes were closed, but through the link between them, he knew how glad she was that he was beside her.

Not long after that, Spencer came into the room. Joe eased his hand from hers and stood. They moved away from the couch.

"Did you find out anything?"

Spencer looked into Joe's face, as if he gazed into his soul. "Our doctors are not certain blood would be beneficial, but they believe it might. They are in agreement that it won't hurt her, and blood should help her build strength."

"What do I need to do?" Visions of long fanged creatures blew through his head, and he pushed them away. This wasn't a late-night creature feature.

Spencer had a little smile on his face that told Joe he probably knew what he was thinking. Hell, the man probably knew what he had for lunch yesterday.

"Relax," Spencer said. "I'm not about to hurt a guy who's helping a good friend of mine."

They walked back to where Veronica lay. Spencer reached for Joe's arm, shoved up his sleeve, and wiped a spot on Joe's wrist.

He tried not to think about what Spencer was doing. "Have you known Veronica long?" Joe asked.

"About ten years. My brother's an anthropologist, and they bonded over science when we all lived in Knoxville. We hung out together until life pushed us in different directions."

He caught a glimpse of an object that looked a lot like a small, sharp knife. Averting his gaze, he focused on helping the woman he loved.

"Look at me," Spencer said. Joe decided he'd better do what the man with the sharp object said. For a second he was drifting. Spencer tugged his arm, and looked down to see Veronica touch her lips to his wrist. A wave swirled through of sensual, erotic tingling. This is wrong, he thought, and tried to push away the sensation.

"What you feel is normal," Spencer said. "My brother calls it adaptive evolution. It helps us find willing donors, and thus assures our survival."

"Isn't the germ transfer dangerous?" Mike asked from the other side of the couch.

"No," Spencer told him. "We are immune to most human germs, and our saliva transfers that to the donor area. The wounds are small, don't get infected, and heal quickly."

"Another adaptation," Mike said, and Spencer nodded.

Joe watched the soft lips on his arm, and his gut knotted. "I can't lose her," he whispered.

"You won't." Mike sounded sure, and Joe wanted to believe that.

Spencer's hand gripped Joe's shoulder.

"Thanks for the support, both of you."

A few minutes later, Veronica released his arm. Spencer wiped her mouth, then cleaned and bandaged Joe's wound. Spencer and Mike went back into the lab area. Joe, grateful for the privacy, pulled a chair next to the couch and took Veronica's hand in his.

****

Veronica's body ached and her mouth was as dry as if it was filled with silica gel. She opened her eyes to find herself on the couch in Dr. Wright's office. Though not surprised, she had hoped maybe the whole being kidnapped and stabbed with a syringe filled with a deadly virus thing was an evil dream fueled by too many pastries from Sweet Bea's. Just the thought of a cherry pastry had her mouth watering.

Blinking to clear her vision, she shifted her position and there was Joe sprawled in a chair beside the couch, his hand holding hers, his body twisted so his head was beside her on the couch. She smiled and touched his soft dark hair.

A moment later, Joe raised his head. "Are you okay?" he asked.

She smiled. "I'm fine. Sorry to wake you."

He stared at her for a moment, then touched the back of his fingers to her forehead. "You're cool."

"I feel better."

"Oh, thank God!" His dark eyes glistened with tears.

Her heart turned over. "I'm sorry I scared you so badly."

"Not your fault." He kissed her forehead, and she pulled him down to touch her lips to his. He was smiling when he moved back.

Her face went hot, and she touched her fingertips to her mouth. "I'm sorry, I'm sure my breath is horrible."

"Don't care," he whispered, as he captured her mouth again with his.

"I take it she's better," Mike said.

Joe finished what he was doing before he spoke. "Much."

"When you two get finished, I'd like to check you out, Veronica."

"Later," she murmured.

When Joe pulled away, she moaned in frustration.

"Better let him make sure you're all right."

The scientist part of her knew an exam by a physician was a necessity. The part that was all woman wanted to tell Mike to get lost and pull Joe on top of her. The men didn't give her a choice.

When Mike finished poking and prodding and asking questions, his relieved expression had her heart beating faster.

"Well," he said, "I'd love to have some lab tests to back me up, but from what I see she's fine." He gave her a stern look. "Take it easy for at least a week."

"Yes, sir," she said, though she figured her grin undermined her words.

"I'll make sure she does," Joe said.

Mike looked skeptical, but he nodded.

"Would it be okay if I went home?" Then she realized. "I don't even know if it's day or night."

"The sun is just setting," Joe said.

Mike nodded. "If you feel up to it, you can go home. Just please take it easy." He shot a look from one to the other, then moved away to allow Joe to return.

She slid her legs off the side of the couch and with Joe's help, pulled herself to a sitting position. Leaning her head against the back of the couch, she said, "Don't think taking it easy will be a problem."

****

An hour later, with a lot of help from Joe, she walked slowly across the lobby of her apartment building. He'd carried her to Spencer's car, but she had refused to allow him to carry her this time. Although, she wondered if that might have been a bad idea. The stairs were looming like the stack of books she'd moved from her old office to the new one.

"Jesus, Mary, Joseph, and the mule! What happened to you?" Tim came rushing down the stairs, hands on his cheeks like the *Home Alone* boy, his voice even higher-pitched than usual. "Are you all right?"

"I'm fine, Tim."

"Thank God," Joe put in.

Tim's eyes widened. "What happened?"

"Let's talk about it upstairs," she said, wondering again if she could make it.

Tim took the other side of her, and between the two strong men, she began to believe she might get to her apartment.

"I'm Tim, Veronica's next door neighbor and BFF. You must be Joe." He leaned toward her and stage whispered, "He's as fine as you said."

Joe's face went red, and she had to force back a laugh. About halfway up the stairs, her legs turned to rubber, and even with all their support, she fought to stay on her feet. Joe scooped her into his arms and carried her the rest of the way.

"Oh my," Tim gasped. "How romantic!"

Tim took the keys, unlocked the door, and the three of them entered her apartment. Joe started toward the bedroom.

"I'd rather stay in here on the couch," she told him.

"Are you sure?"

"Yes."

The men weren't happy until she was tucked in with a pillow and blanket from her bed, though temperature was comfortable.

"Do you need anything?" Joe asked.

Groggy from exertion, she smiled. "Pastry from Sweet Bea's."

"Everything's probably closed, baby."

"I know Julie," Tim said. "Will mini blueberry tarts from her shop be okay?"

She nodded. "Wonderful."

"I'll go then."

Tim headed out, and Joe sat on the edge of the couch next to her. "Rest," he whispered.

She was determined to stay awake, but minutes later, she was asleep.

****

It was a good thing Tim brought back not only pastries, but real food too. Joe had no idea he was so hungry until he tasted what Tim called lobster stew. "This is wonderful."

"I thought you might be hungry, so I went by Maggie's diner too."

"You can have your stew. This stuff is beyond fabulous." Veronica bit into the blueberry tart, closed her eyes, and her expression looked like she'd just had an orgasm.

Joe's mouth went dry. It was all he could do not to throw Tim out the door and see if he couldn't put that expression on her face without the aid of pastries.

A knocking pulled him out of the erotic fantasy. Luckily, Tim went to answer the door. Joe thought the odds of being able to walk weren't good.

Tim introduced himself to the visitor, then said he had a rehearsal to get to and hurried off. Joe smiled when he noticed Tim's voice had lowered an octave.

Spencer greeted Joe, then went over to hug Veronica.

Though reluctant to bring up the subject, Joe was too curious not to ask, "Did Todd survive?"

"Barely. He's in a vampire medical facility right now, and will face charges when he recovers."

"He killed my brother." The words were out before Joe realized he was about to say them.

"I know. I can't discuss what kinds of actions will be taken against him, but I promise he will be punished."

Spencer studied Veronica for a moment. "I'm glad you found the perpetrator, but considering what happened, I'm not sure giving you database access was such a smart move."

Her eyes widened for a moment, then she smiled. "Thank you."

He shook his head. "I almost got you killed."

"Joe would have been killed if you hadn't, and most, if not all the Guardians."

"None of that changes the fact you could have died."

She took his hand in hers. "I'm fine, Spencer. Thank you for risking your life to help me."

"Like I would get you into that mess and leave you to whatever happened." He kissed her cheek.

"What about the humans involved in all this?" she asked.

"We have resources. Again, I can't say much, but they will be handled in an appropriate manner." His expression darkened. "And we will be keeping an eye on the Alliance of True Humanity from now on."

"And Kevin?" Worry pulled at her features.

Spencer smiled. "You made an impression on him. He will get the support and guidance he needs, and I believe he will be a major asset to both the vampire and human worlds."

"I'm glad." Tears glinted in her eyes.

"I have to go." Spencer stood. "I'm glad you're feeling better, Veronica. Take care, both of you."

When he was gone, Joe locked the door, then went over to kiss her cheek. "You need rest."

"What I need is a bath." She looked up into Joe's eyes. "But I don't think I should be in the bathtub alone."

He lowered his head for a moment, forcing himself not to grab her and head for the bathroom. "Sweetheart, you're still not well."

"Which is why I need you to wash my back—or whatever—and make sure I'm all right." She reached over and jerked his shirt free of his jeans. "Wouldn't want your clothes to get wet, now would we?"

"Mike told you to rest."

"So you do all the work." She put her hands around his neck and tugged him down until their lips touched. "Please," she whispered.

"I'll run the bathwater."

She grinned as he pulled loose and went toward the bathroom.

The woman would be the death of him.

And he'd die happy.

****

Veronica lay back in the tub and luxuriated in the cocoon of warm water combined with the feel of Joe's hands. At first his touch was soothing, caring, loving. He soaped her and cared for her as if she were a delicate treasure. Before long, the heat between them flared, and his touch changed. He began to pay special attention to her breasts, soaping them, moving the cloth over one, then the other. Circling slowly, he made his way right up to a nipple, then he'd move to the other one.

He had removed his shirt, and she reached a hand up to his chest. Firm, with a nice mat of dark hair, it was a joy to run a hand over. In retaliation to his teasing touch, she ran a finger over first one, then the other of his flat male nipples, and his breath sucked in hard.

He slid the washcloth down her chest, over her belly, between her thighs, but not quite to the place she most wanted him to touch. "Joe, please," she whispered.

"Please what?"

"You know." She grabbed his jeans and unbuttoned the waist. He tried to move back, but she managed to unzip them before he could.

"You need a bath too," she said, as she tried to get a grip on his pants.

He twisted away before she could. "You think so, do you?"

"Oh yes."

"Are you sure, sweetheart?" The concern in his face warmed her heart.

She tugged at his belt. "Get in here!"

Grinning, he shoved his pants and briefs to the floor. "You sure that tub is big enough for both of us?"

"Let's find out."

With a hand on each side, he lowered his big body into the water. She grabbed the washcloth and began working on his chest, his belly, his legs.

He gasped, and she smiled. "This is fun."

"So is this." He leaned forward and licked one of her nipples, then the other.

By this time, she was having trouble focusing on

what she was doing, but she managed to get a hand on his erection.

He sucked a nipple into his mouth, and she barely managed to hang on to him. He slid his hand between her legs, and she all but lost consciousness. "Joe, please."

"Please what?"

"Make love to me."

"As you wish," he whispered.

He moved her over onto his lap and she maneuvered to the place she most wanted to be. He gently lifted her and slid inside. He held her and did most of the moving. She gripped his shoulders and enjoyed the sensation as they moved toward a mutual release. As they reached climax together, the rest of the world fell away.

****

Hours later, they lay in her bed, her head resting on his shoulder, her body satisfied in a way she'd never known. "I love you," she told him.

He was quiet for a time, and she raised up to look into his face. "Something wrong?"

"No." He brushed the back of his fingers across her cheek. "I was just thinking."

Fear twisted around her heart, making her a little dizzy. "About what?"

"About the chances of a human and a vampire having a committed relationship."

"I have never heard of such a thing," she said. "I guess it would be unexplored territory."

He looked away, then into her eyes. "I know we would face quite a bit of shock and misunderstanding, but I believe in our ability to deal with them. Together.

Long term"

Her heart threatened to thump right out of her chest. "What are you saying?"

"Will you marry me?"

Her breath caught in her chest. She fell back onto the bed and stared at the ceiling. "Do you have any idea how hard it would be?"

"Yes, but I want to spend the rest of my life with you."

"But marriage…"

He rolled onto his side and looked into her eyes. "It would be a challenge, I know."

"We wouldn't belong in either world, and some of my people would object to the point of possible violence—some of yours too." She looked into his eyes. "You've seen what happens when our worlds clash."

"I understand that, but do we have to give up our happiness because of prejudice and misunderstanding." He took her hand in his. "We are not that different."

It was what she'd been arguing for years. She touched the healing wound on his wrist. "Different enough. We are different species, so different foods, different lifestyles. No children."

"You're positive we're different species?"

"Joe, I need blood to survive. You've seen what the sun does to me."

"You research genetics. are there really enough genetic differences to prove we aren't the same species that adapted in different ways?"

She propped her head up and looked at him. "You know that is an almost impossible question to answer."

"How about physiologically, has the different species hypothesis been tested?"

That had her sitting up. "You mean has there ever been a human/vampire child?"

"Yes."

"Not documented." She bit her lip. "But there have been rumors." She put her palm against his face. "Chances are we won't be able to have children."

"Doesn't matter. I love you, Veronica. We can adapt."

Tears welled in her eyes. She wanted to say yes so badly it hurt, but she knew there were a lot of things to consider.

"Just think about it. Okay?"

"Okay." She cuddled next to him and considered how wonderful it sounded to be with him every day, to share their lives. Was it possible marriage between a vampire and human could work? Or was it too much to ask?

And what price would they have to pay to find out?

Chapter 13

"Mike said you need to rest." Joe tucked the light blanket around her. "It's only been two days."

"I feel fine," Veronica told him. "Besides, Mike is a human physician."

Joe leaned down so his nose almost touched hers. "You're the one who's always talking about how alike our species are."

She grabbed him around the neck and leaned up to kiss him. After a breathtaking interval, she backed away enough to whisper. "We do seem to be rather compatible."

They were engaged in another compatibility test when they heard a knock at the door. Joe groaned. "If it's Mike, I'm going to throw him down the stairs."

He went to the door as Veronica giggled.

"Who are you?" A tall, dark-haired woman glared at Joe like he was dirt on a floor she'd just scrubbed.

A shorter, younger woman tried, without success, to shove the older one out of the way. "You must be Joe. I'm Charlene, Veronica's sister. And this," she indicated the older woman, "is Emelda Teal, our mother."

"Nice to meet you both. Veronica's on the couch." He stepped back and waved them toward the living room.

The older Teal blew toward Veronica like an eagle

swooping in for its prey. Joe didn't realize he was staring until a finger poked his arm.

"It's okay, she probably won't eat you."

Charlene's impish grin pulled a tiny smile from him. "You sure?"

She shrugged. "Absolutely maybe."

He shut the door and she walked beside him into the room. "You did good, sis. This guy's a keeper, if Mom doesn't scare him off."

"Charlene!" Mrs. Teal's voice could stop a train. "Do not encourage your sister."

"Okay, that's enough." Veronica held up one hand like she was stopping traffic. "I'm an adult. What I do and who I choose to be with is my business."

Mrs. Teal's nose flared as she gave Veronica a hard stare. "But he's...he's a..."

"Human, Mom." Veronica looked like she wanted to punch something. Or someone. "Joe is human."

The older woman stood, paced a few steps, gave Joe a hard glare, then turned back to Veronica. "Darling, I understand how intriguing they are. Lord knows what I'd do without Fernando, but I would never consider allowing him to exceed his boundaries."

Joe gripped his fists, bit his tongue, and told himself he knew this relationship would be difficult. Still he wasn't sure he could keep his mouth shut.

Fortunately, he didn't have to. "Do you know what you sound like, Mom?" Charlene stomped toward her mother, fists on hips, and face red. "You sound like human slave owners back before the Civil War."

The older woman's face went crimson. "Humans are lesser species. We are their superiors by far."

"I wouldn't be so sure about that," Veronica said.

"Humans and vampires are so similar that some scientists speculate we are one species."

"That's absurd."

"That's what the slave owners said." Charlene glared at her mother.

"I raised both of you better than this. Humans and vampires are totally different. And inferior."

Veronica leaned back and put a hand to her head, and Joe decided he'd had enough. "How about you insult me and my entire species some other time? Right now Veronica needs to rest."

"He's right, Mom." Charlene put a hand on her mother's shoulder. "We need to go."

The woman ignored Charlene and looked toward Veronica. "You never told me what happened, how you got hurt."

"Lab accident," she said.

Mrs. Teal glared at Joe as if she was sure he'd been the cause, but she kissed Veronica's forehead and allowed Charlene to escort her out.

"Are you sure marrying me is a good idea?"

Joe grinned. "Hey, if that's all you've got, just wait until Thanksgiving at the Sullivans'."

"I'm looking forward to it."

Joe shook his head mournfully. "You poor thing."

She grabbed his hand and tugged him down for a kiss. When he sat up, she tried to pull him back.

"You do need to rest."

"What I need is the man I love to make love to me."

"Veronica."

"Please."

Oh hell, he couldn't resist that face.

185

****

A week later, Joe sat at a round table at a little nightclub located somewhere between Lobster Cove and Bar Harbor. Nearby a runway—the kind supermodels use—jutted out to capture a good piece of the floor space. The thing had blue, yellow, purple, and pink lights sending out overlapping ovals of color. The same wild lighting lined the perimeter of the club, painting long streaks of color on the brick walls. Lots of lighting, not much light to see by.

He shifted in his seat. Why had he agreed to come to a place called The Diva Room? Across the table, Spencer was looking uncomfortable too. Joe bit back a smile, if he could tell that poker-faced Guardian was out of his element, the man must be miserable.

"Relax," Veronica said. "This will be fun."

"I've heard of these clubs, but I've never been to one." Mike said. "I've always wondered what they were really like."

Joe turned to look at his buddy, who somehow had managed to land in a seat between Veronica and Charlene. "Maybe Tim will give you some tips on makeup and stuff."

Mike grinned. "That might be fun."

"Lyndsy would be so proud."

"Maybe she'll go shopping with me."

Charlene rolled her eyes. "Tim's a fantastic performer. It'll be great, you'll see."

Joe wondered what other kinds of crazy stuff he'd do for love. Then he looked at Veronica, and decided there was nothing he wouldn't do for her.

The show began, and the first performer took the stage dressed in a shiny pink evening gown, shoes with heels that could be used to kill, and enough jewelry to blind a guy if the light was right. Joe knew there was a man under all the flash and makeup, but without prior knowledge, it would be hard to tell.

The guy launched into a decent rendition of an old Barbra Streisand song, and Joe decided to sit back and try not to be too freaked out by the whole thing.

Veronica knew Joe was not thrilled about being at the club, neither was Spencer for that matter, but she was grateful they had agreed to come with her. She knew it might be a while before they could all be together again.

Beside her, Charlene bounced in her seat. It was good to see her sister enjoying herself.

"We should have invited Mom," Charlene whispered.

She turned to stare at her sister. "Why would you want to do that?"

Charlene giggled. "To see her reaction."

Veronica turned back to the performer, who was just finishing up. As she applauded, she pictured her mother's reaction to these talented human men dressing and acting like beautiful, talented women. By the time the next act came on stage, she was fighting the urge to laugh.

"See," Charlene whispered. "It would be hilarious."

"You're bad."

"Yep."

Veronica turned back to the show with a new appreciation for her sister's sense of humor.

A "Judy Garland," performed, then a "Marilyn Monroe," a "Julie Andrews," a "Cher," and a

"Madonna." All talented and beautiful.

Then came the part they'd all been waiting for. Tim, performing as T-Spot, took the stage.

He was dressed in a rich blue gown with fitted sleeves and a full skirt. Completing the outfit was matching wrap and elbow-length white gloves. He had on a long, black wig pulled back into a perfect up-do.

"Tonight I'm channeling Maria Callas," Tim announced. "I'm singing her version of the aria "Un Bel Di Vedremo" from Puccini's *Madame Butterfly*."

Veronica gasped when he started singing. She'd known Tim for over a year, had seen him perform, but she had no idea the man could do opera.

"What a voice!" Charlene whispered. Murmured agreement came not only from their group, but from surrounding tables.

"She's incredible," someone from across the room said. Veronica had to agree.

When he finished, there was a roar and the crowd came to their feet almost as one.

Tim was wiping tears when Veronica dashed to the stage to give him the dozen red roses she'd bought. He hugged her, and his trembling vibrated through her. "I can't believe this," he whispered.

"Believe it." She kissed his cheek before heading back to her seat.

****

Not quite three hours later, Veronica and Joe met the other three in the park at the center of Lobster Cove. Normally the area would be deserted at almost one in the morning, but the Harvest of the Sea Festival was at its height, so a modest number of folks still wandered about, buying food from vendors, playing games, just enjoying the unseasonably warm night. Joe smiled, and Veronica all but melted.

The group found a couple of black wrought-iron benches that faced each other. Joe put his arm around her and pulled her close.

Tim, sans makeup and wearing a lavender button-down shirt with black slacks, tried hard to keep his lawyer persona going, but he kept bursting into giggles. "Oh my God," he whispered, "I hope nobody from the office sees me tonight."

"I guess it's a good thing you work in Bar Harbor, and not Lobster Cove," Veronica told him.

He rolled his eyes. "Why do you think I live in Lobster Cove instead of Bar Harbor? Makes for fewer problems."

"Forget being a lawyer and take your show on the road," Charlene told him. "You'd make a fortune."

That only provoked another round of giggles.

Joe leaned toward Veronica. "He's happy."

She looked into his eyes. "So am I."

"Really?"

"Oh yeah." She put a hand against his cheek. "In fact, I'm happier than I've ever been."

His lips twitched as if he wanted to smile, but he kept a guarded expression on his face. "Any special reason?"

"Actually, yes. I found my beloved—a huge deal for vampire. Or, to put it another way, the man I love asked me to marry him."

Hope flashed in his eyes. "So, are you thinking about saying yes?"

"No."

His body seemed to collapse forward. The light

went out of his eyes, and his expression was one of sadness. "I understand."

She touched his cheek. "I don't have to think about it anymore. I've decided I can't imagine not having you in my life. I'd be honored to be your beloved—your wife. So, yes."

He stood, pulling her to her feet at the same time. He kissed her within an inch of her life, then swung her around in a circle.

"What the hell are you doing?" Mike asked. His voice was gruff, but his lips edged toward a smile.

Joe grinned. "She said yes. She said she'd marry me!"

There was a moment of stunned silence, then a cheer went up, not only from their group, but from people close enough to hear. "Congratulations," sounded from all around them. Cell phones and cameras raised to snap photos.

Charlene grabbed them both in a big hug. "I'm so happy for you two."

Mike slapped Joe on the back so hard Joe took a step forward. "You will have the best bachelor party ever."

Tim was crying. "I'm so happy for you," he managed, then dissolved into tears again.

A hand touched her shoulder, and she turned to see Spencer standing beside her, concern in his expression. "Are you sure about this?"

"Positive."

"Then I'm happy for both of you." He hugged her. "If you need me, just call."

"Thank you." she wiped at a tear that had escaped her efforts not to cry.

The party involved at least half the festival crowd, everybody laughing and dancing around trees, and benches, and flower beds, and the little water fountain with its tiny concrete pond. The celebration lasted until almost dawn, but before the sun became an issue, the group went their separate ways. Tim headed to his apartment, Spencer escorted Charlene to hers. Mike went to the apartment that had been Justin's.

Veronica and Joe went to her apartment for some alone time. Once inside, Joe pulled her close. "Are you sure marriage is what you want?"

She smiled. "Yes, I'm sure. You?"

"Oh yeah." He sighed, the thought of leaving her now was almost more than he could handle. "I guess I need to go back to Tennessee and finish the semester."

"I'm thinking of taking some time off," she said. "I have a feeling the lab will be shut down while they investigate what Todd did—and clean up his mess."

"I like that idea." He took her hand. "I'll have to find out if any colleges around here need a new teacher."

"Or you could work at the lab."

He stared. "Somehow I don't think that will work."

"Other labs have humans and vampires working side by side."

"They probably have special skills your people find useful."

"Your skills would be useful."

He kissed her cheek. "Thank you for your faith in me."

"You were strictly a research scientist before you took your teaching position, right"

"Yes." He narrowed his eyes. "Did you read that in

my mind?"

She laughed her clear, sparkling laugh. "No, I Googled you, silly."

"Did you now?"

"Yes, and I see in your mind that you want to get back to pure research." she frowned. "Why did you start teaching in the first place, if you dislike it so?"

"Ex-wife," he told her. "I thought changing jobs would save our marriage. I was mistaken. And, before you ask, I guess I stayed at the university because it was easier than to look for a new job. Teaching isn't so bad."

"But not your true calling." Her bright eyes searched his. "I want you to be happy."

He grinned. "Know what would make me happy?"

"I'll bet I can guess."

"Then let's celebrate some more."

He swept her into his arms and headed to the bedroom.

A word about the author...

Cheryel Hutton is a dragon whisperer. She can hear dragons when they tell her fantastic stories. Sometimes they tell her stories about humans and their adventures. Sometimes the stories are about bigfoot, or werewolves, or aliens. Sometimes, the dragons even tell stories about other dragons. There is really no way of knowing what tales the dragons are going to tell next. Cheryel writes down what the dragons tell her, and shares the tales with all who want to read them.

Cheryel has two beautiful, talented daughters and several extremely adorable grandchildren. She lives near Jacksonville, Florida with her husband, two dachshunds, and a muse named Quill who, of course, is a dragon. She is the author of *Keepers of Legend*, *The Ugly Truth*, and *Secrets of Ugly Creek*, all published by The Wild Rose Press, Inc.

www.cheryelhutton.com
www.dragonwhisperer.me

Thank you for purchasing
this publication of The Wild Rose Press, Inc.

If you enjoyed the story, we would appreciate your
letting others know by leaving a review.

For other wonderful stories,
please visit our on-line bookstore at
www.thewildrosepress.com.

For questions or more information
contact us at
info@thewildrosepress.com.

The Wild Rose Press, Inc.
www.thewildrosepress.com

Stay current with The Wild Rose Press, Inc.

Like us on Facebook
https://www.facebook.com/TheWildRosePress

And follow us on Twitter
https://twitter.com/WildRosePress